Margaret Veley

Mitchelhurst Place
Volume II

Outlook

Margaret Veley

Mitchelhurst Place
Volume II

1. Auflage | ISBN: 978-3-73262-345-7

Erscheinungsort: Frankfurt am Main, Deutschland

Erscheinungsjahr: 2018

Outlook Verlag GmbH, Frankfurt.

Margaret Veley

Mitchelhurst Place
Volume II

Outlook

MITCHELHURST PLACE
VOL. II

MITCHELHURST PLACE

A Novel

BY

MARGARET VELEY

AUTHOR OF "FOR PERCIVAL"

"Que voulez-vous? Hélas! notre mère Nature,

Comme toute autre mère, a ses enfants gâtés,

Et pour les malvenus elle est avare et dure!"

IN TWO VOLUMES
VOL. II.

London
MACMILLAN AND CO.
1884

The Right of Translation and Reproduction is Reserved.

Bungay:
CLAY AND TAYLOR, PRINTERS.

MITCHELHURST PLACE

CHAPTER I.
NO LETTER.

The Mitchelhurst postman, coming up to the Place in his daily round, found a young man loitering to and fro within view of the gate. The morning was a pleasant one. The roadside grass was grey with dew, and glistening pearls and diamonds were strung on the threads of gossamer, tangled over bush and blade. The hollies in the hedgerows were brave and bright, and there were many-tinted leaves yet clinging to the bramble-sprays. Sun and wet together had turned the common road to a shining, splendid way, up which the old postman crept, a dull, little, toiling figure, with a bag over his shoulder, and something white in his hand. The young man timed his indolent stroll so that they met each other on the weedy slope, which led to the iron gate, with its solid pillars, and white stone balls. There, with the briefest possible nod by way of salutation, he demanded his letters.

The old fellow knew him as the gentleman who was staying with Mr. Hayes, and touched his cap obsequiously. He had carried his bag for more than thirty years, and remembered old Squire Rothwell, and Mr. John, and he fumbled with the letters in his hand, half expecting a curse at his slowness, and hardly knowing what name he was to look for. The other stood with his head high, showing a sharply-cut profile as he turned a little, looking intently in the direction of the Place. Through the black bars shone a pale bright picture of blue sky, and level turf, and the gnarled and fantastic branches of the sunlit avenue. There were yellow leaves on the straight roadway, and shadows softly interlaced, and at the end the white, silent house.

The postman finished his investigation, and announced in a hesitating tone, "No, sir, no letter, sir. No letter at all, name of Rothwell."

The young man turned upon him. "Harding, I said."

"Yes, sir. No, sir, no letter name of Harding."

"Are you sure? Give them to me."

He looked them over. There were letters and papers for Mr. Hayes, one or two for the servants, and one that had come from Devonshire for Barbara. He gave them back with a meditative frown, and turned on his heel without a word. The postman pushed the gate just sufficiently to permit of a crab-like entrance to the grounds, and plodded along the avenue, while the young fellow walked definitely away towards the village.

"The old boy doesn't write business letters on Sunday, I dare say," he said to himself. "No, I don't suppose he would. Well, I shall hear to-morrow. As well to-morrow as to-day, perhaps—better, perhaps. And yet—and yet—Oh God! to get to work! I have banished myself from her presence, I have shut that gate against me—that old fool goes crawling up there with his letters—any one in Mitchelhurst may knock at that door, and I may not! There's nothing left for me but to do the task she set me, and by Heaven, I will! I shall have the right to speak to her then, at any rate!"

Barbara had intended to see Reynold before he left that morning. She did not know what she wanted to say, she was uneasy at the thought of the interview, but she could not endure that he should be dismissed from the old house without a parting word. While Harding was moodily doubting whether he had not alienated her for ever, she was wondering what she could say or do to atone for the wrong done to him by her timidity. She did not fully understand the meaning of the wrathful anguish of his last speech, but she knew that she had pained him. She planned a score of dialogues, she wearied herself in vain endeavours to guess what he would say, and then, tired out, she solved the question by sleeping till the sunlight fell upon her face, and the banished man was already beyond the gate.

She knew the truth the moment she awoke. It was only to confirm her certainty that she dressed hurriedly and went out into the passage, to see the door standing wide, and the vacant room. It seemed but yesterday, and yet so long ago, since she made it ready for the coming guest, who had left it in anger. Barbara sighed, and turned away. At the head of the stairs she recalled the slim, dark figure that had stood there so few hours before, fixing his angry eyes upon her, and grasping the balustrade with long fingers as he spoke. The very ticking of the old clock reminded her of their talk together the morning after he came, and seemed to say "gone! gone! gone! gone!" as she went by.

Her uncle came down a few minutes later, greeted her shortly, and glanced at the table. It was laid for two. "I suppose there is nothing to wait for?" he said.

"Nothing," said Barbara, and she rang the bell.

He unfolded a newspaper and spoke from behind it. "You know that young fellow is gone?"

"Yes."

"Time he did go! I wish he had never come! Did you say good-bye to him?"

"No. He went before I was down."

Mr. Hayes uttered a little sound expressive of satisfaction, and the girl perceived that she had accidentally led him to suppose that she had had no talk with Harding since the quarrel. She did not speak. The maid came into the room with the urn, and Mr. Hayes turned to her. "What man was that I saw in the hall just now?"

"He came for the gentleman's portmanteau, sir. He was to take it to Mrs. Simmonds."

He started, but controlled himself. "Mrs. Simmonds?"

"Yes, sir, Mrs. Simmonds at the shop."

Mr. Hayes was silent only till the door was closed behind her. Then, "He has done that to spite me!" he said furiously. "Serves me right for trying to be civil to one of these confounded Rothwells! They have the devil's own temper, every one of them, and if they can do you a bad turn, they will!"

Barbara said nothing, but made tea rather drearily.

"Confound him!" Mr. Hayes began afresh. "Now I suppose the whole place will be cackling about this! He deserves to be kicked out of the parish, and I should like to do it! I wish to heaven, Barbara, you wouldn't pick young men out of the ditches in this fashion! You see what comes of it!"

Barbara, appealed to in this direct and reasonable manner, plucked up her spirit, and replied, rather loftily, that she would certainly remember in future. She further remarked that the fish was getting cold.

Mr. Hayes threw down the paper, and took his place. There was silence for a minute or two, and then he began again.

"There isn't a soul in Mitchelhurst that doesn't know he was staying here. What do you suppose they will say when they find him starting off at a moment's notice, and taking a lodging in the village, not a stone's throw from my gate?"

Barbara privately thought that, as Mr. Harding had betaken himself to the further end of Mitchelhurst, her uncle's talent for throwing stones must be remarkable. She did not suggest this, however, and when he repeated his question, "What do you suppose they will say?" she only replied that she did not know, she was sure.

"Don't you?" said he, with withering scorn. "Well, I do." It was true enough. He could guess pretty well what the gossips would say, and the sting of it was that their version would not differ very much from the actual fact.

Barbara looked down, and finished her breakfast without a word. She knew that silence was the safest course she could adopt, since it gave him no chance of turning his anger on her, but she also knew that it irritated him dreadfully. That, however, she did not mind. Barbara herself was rather cross that

7

morning. She had meant to be up early, and she had slept later than usual; she was vexed and disappointed, and she had been worried by the jarring tempers of the last two days. She kept her head bent, and her lips closed, while Mr. Hayes drank his second cup of tea with a muttered accompaniment of abuse.

"Look here," he said suddenly, getting up, and going to the fire, "I don't know how long that fellow means to stay in Mitchelhurst, but, till he leaves, you don't go beyond the gate. I don't suppose you would wish to do so"—he paused, but she was apparently absorbed in the consideration of a little ring on her finger—"I should hope you have proper feeling enough not to wish to do so"—this appeal was also received in a strictly neutral manner—"but in any case you have my express command to the contrary."

"Very well," said Barbara, with a little affectation of being rather weary of the whole subject.

"I do not choose that you should be exposed to insult," Mr. Hayes continued.

"Very well," said Barbara again. "I can stay in if you like, though I don't think Mr. Harding would insult me."

"I beg your pardon, my dear, but you are not qualified to judge in this matter. If you had heard Mr. Harding's conversation last night you might not be quite so sure what he would or would not do. It is my duty to protect you from an unpleasant possibility, and you will oblige me by not going beyond—or rather by not going near the gate."

Barbara, tired of saying "Very well," said "All right."

"Wednesday is the night of Pryor's entertainment at the schools. I shall be sorry to disappoint him, but I certainly shall not go unless Mr. Harding has left the place. He has shown such a deplorable want of taste and proper feeling that he would probably take that opportunity of thrusting himself upon us."

Mr. Hayes paused once more, but the girl did not seem inclined either to defend or to denounce their late guest. She changed her position listlessly, and gazed out of the window.

"A gentleman would not, but that proves nothing with regard to Mr. Harding. You are very silent this morning, Barbara."

"I have a headache," she said, "I'm tired," and to her great relief, Mr. Hayes, after walking two or three times up and down the room, went off to his study.

The poor little man was not happy. He sincerely regretted the quarrel of the evening before, which had come upon him, as upon Reynold, unawares. He was accustomed to the society of a few neighbours, who understood him, and said behind his back, "Oh, you must not mind what Hayes says!" or "I met Hayes yesterday—a little bit more cracked than usual!" and took all his sallies good-humouredly, with argument, perhaps, or loud-voiced denial at the time, but nothing in the way of consequences. Thunder might roll, but no bolt fell, and the sky was as clear as usual at the next meeting. Mr. Hayes had unconsciously fallen into the habit of talking without any sense of responsibility. On this occasion a variety of circumstances had combined to irritate him, and his personal dislike of Reynold Harding had given a touch of acrid malice to his attack, but he meant no more than to have the pleasure of contradicting, and, if possible, silencing his companion. The game was played more roughly than usual, but Mr. Hayes never realised that his adversary was angrily in earnest till it was too late. Excitement had mastered him, there was an interchange of speeches, swift and fierce as blows, and then he saw Kate Rothwell's son, standing before him, trembling with fury, and hoarsely declaring that he would leave the house at once. He had only to close his eyes to see him again, the tall young figure leaning forward into the light, with his clenched hands resting on the polished table, amid the disarray of silver and glasses, his dark brows drawn down, and his angry eyes aglow. Conciliation was impossible on either side, though the shock of definite rupture so far sobered them that Harding's departure was deferred to the morning. But, "I will never break bread under *your* roof again!" the young man had said, with a glance round the room, and a curious significance of tone. Then he turned away to encounter Barbara upon the stairs.

To Harding, matters had seemed at their worst during the black hours of silence, and the morning brought something of comfort. If there is but a possibility that work may help us in our troubles, the dullest day is better than the night. But to Mr. Hayes the daylight came drearily, showing the folly of a business which nothing could mend. For more than a quarter of a century he had plumed himself on his gratitude to Kate Rothwell for her kindness to his dead love, and had imagined that he only lacked an opportunity to serve her. And this graceful sentiment, being put to the test, had not prevented him from quarrelling with her son, and turning the young fellow out of doors. Yes, he, Herbert Hayes, had actually driven Kate's boy from Mitchelhurst Place! and what made it worse, if anything could make it worse, was the revelation of the utter impotence of that cherished gratitude. He regretted what he had done, but he must abide by it. Apologise to Harding?—he would die first! Own to one of the Rothwells that he had been in the wrong?—the mere thought, crossing his mind, as he tied his cravat that morning, very nearly choked him. Never— never! Not if it were Kate herself! But he reddened to the roots of his white hair at the thought of the gossip and laughter which would follow the unseemly squabble.

He would be unfairly judged. He said so over and over again, and in a certain sense it was true, for he had never intended to quarrel with his guest. But he could not prove even the innocence he felt. He remembered two or three bitter fragments of their wrangling which would condemn him if repeated. Yet he knew he had not meant them as his judges would take them. "Well, but," some practical neighbour would say, "if you say such things, what do you expect?" That was just it—he had expected nothing, though nobody would believe it, and all at once this catastrophe had come upon him.

So he went down to breakfast, sincerely troubled and repentant, and consequently in a very unpleasant mood. Repentance seldom makes a man an agreeable companion, and when it seizes the head of the house the subordinate members naturally share his discomfort. The moment he set foot in the breakfast-room he was met by the news of Harding's stay in the village, and his anger blazed up again, though, through it all, he had an uncomfortable consciousness that the young man had a right to stay in Mitchelhurst if he pleased. If he could only have convinced himself that Reynold was utterly in the wrong, he would have forgiven him and been happy. But it is almost impossible to forgive a man who is somewhat in the wrong, yet less so than oneself.

Harding had been guided by Barbara in his search for a lodging. When they were standing together at the edge of the ditch, she had reminded her uncle that Mrs. Simmonds had let her rooms to a man who came surveying. The fact was so unprecedented that the good woman might be pardoned for imagining herself an authority on what gentlemen liked, and what gentlemen expected, on the strength of that one experience. Harding confirmed her in her innocent belief by agreeing to everything she proposed. Within half an hour of his arrival he was sitting down to what the surveyor always took for breakfast, and the surveyor's favourite dinner was cooking for him as he walked fast and far on the first road that presented itself. He almost reached Littlemere before he turned, and had to scramble over a hedge, to avoid what might have been an awkward meeting with Mr. Masters. The little squire went by unsuspectingly, though Reynold, finding himself face to face with a bull in the meadow, nearly jumped back upon him. Happily however the bull took time to consider, and before he had made up his mind whether he liked his visitor or not, the coast was clear, and the young man sprang down into the road, and set off on his way back to Mitchelhurst, where he arrived just as Mrs. Simmonds was beginning to look out for him. The surveyor had ordered rather an early dinner.

Harding had done his best to check any gossip about his affairs, but his landlady was burning with curiosity. She made a remark about Mr. Hayes as she set the dish on the table, and her lodger replied that it certainly was a queer fancy for a lonely man to live in that great house, and might he trouble Mrs. Simmonds for a fork? She supplied the omission with many apologies, and said that Mr. Hayes was not very popular in the neighbourhood, she believed.

"Isn't he?" said Reynold, slicing away. "Well, all I can say is that I found him a very hospitable old gentleman. He had never seen me before, and he invited me to stay there for three days. Wouldn't take any denial."

"Well, to be sure, sir, we can but speak as we find," said Mrs. Simmonds, handing the potatoes. "Only, you see, there are some of us who remember the old family—you'll excuse me, sir, but it's wonderful how you favour Mr. John—and it's not the same, sir, having a stranger there. It's *not* like old times."

"No," said Reynold with a jarring little laugh. "I should think it was a good deal better. Thank you, Mrs. Simmonds, I have all I want."

And with a nod, which was exactly Mr. John's, he dismissed the old lady.

She was disconcerted; she did not know what to make of this young man with the Rothwell features, who was not gratified by a respectful allusion to the family. "A good deal better!" Well, of course, the Rothwells held themselves very high, and thought other people were just the dirt under their feet. There was no pleasing them with anything you sent in, nothing was good enough, and they expected you to stand curtseying and curtseying for their custom, and to wait for your money till all the profit was gone. Mr. Hayes paid as soon as the bill was sent in, and Miss Strange was a pleasant-spoken young lady. "A good deal better"—well, no doubt it was.

And yet the good woman had not been insincere when she spoke of the old times with a regretful accent in her voice. She remembered John Rothwell's father as a middle-aged gentleman, alert and strong. Those old times were the times when she was a rosy-cheeked girl, whom Simmonds came courting at her father the wheel-wright's, and not Simmonds only, for she might have done better if she had chosen. It was in the good old times that they set up their little shop, and that their little girl was born who had been in the churchyard three-and-twenty years come Christmas. There were no times now like those before Mitchelhurst Place was sold, when she didn't know what rheumatism was, and there were none of your new-fangled Board Schools, to teach children to think little of their elders. It was not to be supposed that Mrs. Simmonds thought that her stiff old joints would become flexible again if the Rothwells came back to the manor-house, but she certainly felt that in their reign the world went its way with fewer obstructions and less weariness, and was more brightly visible without the aid of spectacles. She had an impression, too, that the weather was better.

She straightened herself laboriously after taking the apple-pie from the oven, and was horrified to find the crust a little caught on one side. Having to explain how this had occurred when she carried it in, she had no opportunity of continuing the previous conversation, and the moment dinner was over Reynold was out again. The fact was that Mrs. Simmonds's parlour, which was small and low, and had been carefully shut up for many months, was not very attractive to the young man, who was fresh from the faded stateliness of the old Place. Besides, he was anxious to keep down importunate thoughts by sheer weariness, if in no other way.

He went that afternoon to the Hall, the dreary old farmhouse which Barbara had pointed out as the Rothwells' earlier home, and walked in the sodden pastures where she picked her cowslips in the spring. He looked more kindly at the old house, in spite of the ignoble disorder of its surroundings, but he lingered longest at the gate where she had shown him Mitchelhurst, spread out before him like the Promised Land. He studied it all in the fading light, and then, with a farewell glance at the white far-off front of the Place, he went down into the village, tired enough to drop asleep over the fire after tea.

"To-morrow, the letter," was his last thought as he lay down.

CHAPTER II.
ONE MORE HOLIDAY.

The inevitable morning came, but the letter did not.

Harding was first incredulous, then when a light flashed upon him, he was at once amused and indignant.

"So! I kept you waiting till the latest day, and you are returning the compliment. I am given to understand that you can take your time as well as I? That's fair enough, no doubt, only it seems rather a small sort of revenge, and, as things have turned out, it's a nuisance. What is to be done now? Shall I wait another day for my instructions, or shall I go up to town at once? I told him to write here, but, after all, what is there to say, except, 'Be at the office on such a day?' Shall I go, or stay?"

He tossed up, not ill-pleased to decide his uncle's affairs so airily. The coin decreed that he should stay.

"It's just as well," he said to himself. "I don't want to seem impatient if he isn't."

But the additional day of idleness proved very burdensome. He fancied that the Mitchelhurst gossips watched his every movement; he felt himself in a false position; he shut himself up in his little sitting-room and asked for books. Mrs. Simmonds brought him all she had, but she looked upon reading as a penitential occupation for Sundays, and periods of affliction, and the volumes were well suited for the purpose. Harding thrust them aside. The local paper was nearly a week old, but he read every word of it.

"There'll be a new one to-morrow, sir," said his landlady, delighted to see that he enjoyed it so much.

"Thank you, Mrs. Simmonds, but I shall be far enough away by this time to-morrow," the young man replied.

He spent a considerable part of the afternoon lying on the horse-hair couch, and staring at the ceiling. A ceiling is not, as a rule, very interesting to study, and the only thing that could be said for this one was that it was conveniently near. Reynold could examine every smoke-stain at his ease, and every fly that chanced to stroll across his range of vision. The first he noticed made him think of Barbara and Joppa, but the later comers were simply wearisome. There is a distressing want of individuality about flies. Even when one buzzed about his head, with a fixed determination to wander awhile upon his forehead, he had not an idea which fly it was. It seemed to him, as he lay there, with his arm thrown up for a pillow, that flies in general were just one instrument of torture of, say, a billion-fly power The afternoon sunshine and the smouldering fire had wakened more than he could reckon in the little parlour.

He would not have cared to confess how much he was troubled by his uncle's silence. He had expected to be met rather more than half-way, instead of which it seemed that he was to be taught to know his place. The idea was intolerable, and it haunted him.

When Mrs. Simmonds came in with a tray (the surveyor always took his tea between five and six), she made a remark or two about things in general, which Reynold, turning his lustreless eyes upon her, endeavoured to receive with a decent show of interest. When she brought the tea-pot, she told him that Mr. Hayes had sent to the Rothwell Arms for a carriage early that afternoon. "Indeed!" said Reynold, this time endeavouring to conceal the interest he felt.

"What were they going to do?" he wondered, as he propped his head on his hand and sipped his tea. Was the old man taking Barbara away? What did it mean?

It meant simply that Mr. Hayes had wearied of his self-imposed seclusion, and had announced to his niece that he should drive over to Littlemere and see Masters. He added that he might not return to dinner, and that she was not to wait for him. While Reynold lay on the sofa the carriage had gone by, with the little man sitting in it, his head rather more bowed than usual, planning how he would explain the quarrel to his friend. "Masters will understand—he knows how the fellow behaved the night before," said Mr. Hayes to himself a score of times. But every time he said it he felt a little less certain that Masters would understand exactly as he wished.

Mrs. Simmonds, returning after a considerable interval, told her lodger that the wind was getting up, and she thought there was going to be a change in the weather. She mostly knew, as she informed him, on account of her rheumatism. Reynold opened the door for her and her tray, and then went to the window.

The moon had risen, the low roofs and gaunt poplars of Mitchelhurst were black in its light, and wild wreaths of cloud were tossed across the sky. It was a sky that seemed to mean something, to have a mood and expression of its own. Reynold watched it for a few minutes, till its vastness made the little box of a room, where even the flies had fallen asleep again, insupportably small. He took his hat and went out.

He did not care which way he went, if only it were not in the direction of the Place. Mr. Hayes, when he charged Barbara not to go near the gate, had a sort of fancy that the young fellow might walk defiantly on the very edge of the forbidden ground, and peer through the bars with a white, spiteful face. The girl acquiesced indifferently. She might not altogether understand Reynold Harding, but she knew most certainly that he would never approach them.

It chanced that evening that he took a narrow lane which led out of the Littlemere road. It proved to be a rugged but very gradual ascent. Presently it led him through a gate, and, still gently rising, became a mere cart track across open fields, where the wind came in sudden, hurrying gusts over the grey slopes, and brought undefinable suggestions of hopelessness and solitude. Reaching the highest point the wayfarer passed through another gate, and pursued a level road, bordered by spaces of unenclosed grass, sometimes widening almost to a common, sometimes shrinking to a mere strip between the white way and the low hedgerows. Reynold pushed forward, gazing at the sky. The clouds, torn and driven by the wind, fled wildly overhead, like shattered squadrons, and yet rolled up in new unconquered masses, as if from a gloomy host encamped on the horizon. The moon, slowly climbing the heavens, fought her way as a swimmer fights the waves. Now she would show a pale face through the blanched ripples of a misty sea, then would be over-powered by a black deluge of cloud, which darkened earth and sky, and swept over her sunken and scarcely suspected presence. And then suddenly she would emerge, pearl-white and pure, from the midst of the fierce confusion, rising unopposed over a gulf of shadowy blue. Or yet again she would glance mockingly from behind a rent veil of gossamer at the lonely little traveller who toiled so far below, under the vast arch of the heavens, and who raised his pre-occupied eyes to her, from the world of dream and mystery which he carried with him under the little arch of his skull. To Harding just then that inner world seemed more real, stranger, and less trodden, than did the world without. The billows of cloud, vast and formless and dark, rolling on high, were no more than symbols of the undefined forebodings which gathered blackly in his soul and changed with every thought. The wild and restless melancholy of the evening harmonised so marvellously with his temper, that he could almost have forgotten its outward reality, had it not been for the wind which blew freshly in his face. It did not seem possible that, when hereafter he came back to Mitchelhurst, he could walk this way whenever he pleased.

Yet he noted landmarks now and then. Here was a thin row of firs, slim and black, then a bare stretch of road where he stepped quickly, his shadow at his side for company, and then a sturdy oak, with all its brown leaves astir in a gust, which whispered hurriedly as he went by. Somewhat further yet the way grew narrow, dipping down into a little hollow, where a runnel of clear water crossed it, glancing over the pebbly earth. There was a plank at one side, and Reynold, stepping on it, smelt the water-mint which clustered at its edge. It seemed, somehow, as if the night, which uttered his desolate thoughts in the wind and the flying clouds, breathed them in that perfume.

Reynold was one of those who take little interest, even as children, in stories of goblins and witches, yet who sympathise with the mood which gave such legends birth, something which in its unshapen darkness and mystery is more impressive than the strangest vision. Why this inexplicable mood, with its world-wide suggestiveness, should have come upon him that evening, transforming the bit of upland country through which he walked to a grey and ghostly region, he could not tell. He tried to reason with his shadowy presentiments. He was going to his work the next day; that very evening he was going back to the little parlour over the shop; Mrs. Simmonds would have his supper ready, old Simmonds would be smoking bad tobacco in the back room; his walk would lead to nothing else. Yet he could not convince himself. He could call up his uncle and Mrs. Simmonds before his eyes, but they were grotesque apparitions in his cloudland. What was it that he was awaiting? Why did he feel as if the crisis of his fate were come, as if it would be upon him before the night were over? "Are we to see it out together?" he said, looking up at the moon.

He hardly knew whether he had uttered the question aloud or not, and he stopped short. There was a pool close by, roughly fenced from the road, and fringed with ragged bushes on the further side. He sat down on the rail. "To-morrow," he said to himself, "nothing can happen before to-morrow." He took old Mr. Harding's letter from his pocket, and tried to read it in the moonlight, but a sudden gust caught it, and almost tore it out of his hand. He crushed the flapping paper together, put it back, and sat gazing at the black pool at his side, idly wondering whether it were deep enough to drown a man. It looked deep, he thought—as deep as the heavens, and a troubled gleam of moonlight rested on it every now and then. Harding knew well that he should never touch his life, yet he played that night with the fancy that in one of the darkened moments when the moon was hidden, it would not be difficult to drop below that shadowy surface, and effectually end the business, so that when the bright glance rested there again it should read nothing. He fancied the moon-beams travelling swiftly along the road, and not finding him, while he lay hidden under the water, with a clump of osiers bending and quivering above him in the windy night. "Why couldn't I do it?" he asked himself. "Why do I go on to meet my ill-luck? It is coming, I know, to play me some devil's trick—I feel it in the air, just as Mrs. Simmonds feels a change of the weather in her poor bones."

17

So, idly jesting, he stooped and tossed a pebble into the brimming blackness, and as he did so he pictured to himself the groping hands, and the ugly strangling fight with death which the moon might chance to see, if it tore its veil aside too quickly. And, besides, there was the grim uncertainty of it. *What was under that dusky surface?* "That's as you please to put it, I suppose," said Reynold, getting to his feet. "Eternity, or just a little black mud. And, by Jove, that railing's rather shaky!" He turned his face towards Mitchelhurst, laughing at his own folly. "Well, I'll take to-morrow and its chance of fortune— presentiments and all?"

The wind, which had fought against him as he came, seemed now so impatient to get him safely back to Mrs. Simmonds, that it fairly took him by the shoulders and hurried him along, as if it knew that it was between nine and ten, and that the good lady was addicted to early hours. And perhaps Reynold himself was slightly ashamed of his moonlit vagary, and not altogether unwilling to seek the shelter of that little roof. He ran and walked down the field path, and saw the glimmering lights of the village below, small sparks of friendly welcome in the great night. When, finally, he turned into the Littlemere road, and was somewhat sheltered from the wind, he met a couple of youths, fresh from the "Rothwell Arms," harmonious in their desire to sing together, but not in the result of their efforts. About a hundred yards further he encountered the Mitchelhurst policeman. The road was quite populous and homely.

He had outstripped his forebodings in his hurried race, and the question whether his landlady would think that he was very late for supper was uppermost in his mind. He opened the door, which was never fastened till Simmonds bolted it at night, and drew a breath which gave him a comprehensive idea of the variety of goods they kept in stock. With the chilly sweetness of the night air still upon him, the young man strode into his room, and confronted Barbara Strange, who rose from the sofa to meet him.

All his misgivings overtook him in a moment.

CHAPTER III.
MOONSHINE.

"Miss Strange!" he exclaimed, amazed.

"Oh!" cried Barbara, "I thought you would *never* come!"

"You wanted me! You have been waiting for me! If I had known——" And while he spoke the strangest thoughts and possibilities shaped themselves in his brain, and died away again. If her presence called them up it also killed them. He saw that she was frightened. Her lip quivered, and her eyes looked larger and a little vague. She was gazing at him through a bright film of unshed tears.

"If I had known," he repeated confusedly, as he stepped forward. "What is it?"

They had not shaken hands in his first astonishment, and now she still looked up at him, and his hand dropped unheeded.

"I don't know what you will say to me," she began. "I am so very, very sorry —I felt I must come myself and ask you to forgive me."

"*I* forgive *you*! Why," said Reynold, his eyes shining, "it is you who should forgive!"

Barbara started, and the hot tears dropped, and slid over her burning blushes. She turned away, but too late to hide them. "What do you mean?" she said. "You don't know. I haven't told you yet. What do you suppose I have come for like this? What do you mean?"

He drew back as if he were stung.

"Well, what is it then?"

She threw two letters on the table.

"Letters? You came with those? Upon my word Miss Strange, it's very kind ——"

He stopped short, looking from the letters to her and back again. Barbara shrank away, drawing herself together, but she resolutely fixed her eyes upon his face.

"Why—why—" stammered Harding, turning as pale as death, and then he dropped into a chair and began to laugh.

The letter that lay nearest to him was directed "R. Harding, Esq." in his own handwriting.

"It is my fault!" cried Barbara. "Tell me what I have done! It is something that matters very much! I knew it—I felt it was, the moment I found them. I came with them directly—I was so afraid you might have gone away. Don't laugh! Oh I know it matters dreadfully!"

Harding had had time to master himself.

"On the contrary," he said, "it doesn't matter at all."

He threw himself back in his chair, tilting it carelessly, and looking at Barbara.

"Doesn't it?" said the girl incredulously. "Doesn't it really?"

"Not a bit; why should it? How did it happen?"

Since everything was lost, he might as well hear her talk.

"It was my fault," Barbara repeated, still doubtfully. "I told you to put them on the hall table—it was the day we had those people to dinner."

Reynold nodded.

"I had my apron on, I was busy. I went out to speak to the gardener, and I thought I would give them to the boy, so I put them in my apron pocket, yours and one of mine, and I never thought of them again."

He had balanced his chair very dexterously, and was still looking at her.

"And they have been in that little apron pocket of yours ever since! Dear me, Miss Strange, I hope yours wasn't an important letter. I'm sorry for your correspondent."

"No, mine didn't matter. Mr. Harding, tell me about yours—tell me the truth! All the time I have been waiting here—and I thought you never *would* come! —I have felt more and more sure that yours *did* matter. I can't tell why, but I am certain. Let me know the worst, please. Tell me what I have done!"

"I don't know why you are so determined that you must have done something dreadful. I assure you I'm not in the habit of writing such terribly important letters as you seem to suppose."

Reynold, as he spoke, had been thinking how strange it was that people should excite themselves about their plans for the future. What child's play and chance it all was! You dreamed, and schemed, and worked it all out, you made allowance for everything except what was really going to happen, and suddenly it was all over, and there was nothing more to be said or done. Here, for instance, was Mitchelhurst Place blown away like a bubble! Possibly, somewhere, there might be found something in the shape of a house, a certain quantity of stone and timber, set on the face of the earth and called by that name, but had Reynold been opposite the gate at that moment he would have looked at it with indifference. *His* Mitchelhurst Place, the one he had thought about so much, the one he meant to give the best years of his life to win, was, it now appeared, a house of cards. Barbara and he had been mightily interested in setting it up, and really it had been a very lofty and presentable edifice, till Barbara forgot to put a letter in the post, and so it all tumbled down in a minute. It was a pity, certainly.

"Tell me the truth," said the girl's voice again, with its soft accent of entreaty.

"But you won't believe me! I tell you again, Miss Strange, it doesn't matter a bit. And again, if you like! And again!"

She looked fixedly at him, and stretched out her hand towards the letters.

"Very well," she said. "Shall I post these for you as I go back?"

He brought down his tilted chair with sudden emphasis, and sprang up.

"No!"

He had lost all, but at least his pride was safe. His mother and old Mr. Harding need never learn how nearly they had had their way. He knew what deadly offence he had given by the silence which would be taken for a calculated insult, but he would a thousand times rather face their anger than appeal to their pity with a lame story of a letter delayed. Besides, it was too late. Old Harding was a man of his word, the place was filled up, the chance was gone.

"No!" cried Reynold.

"There!" the girl exclaimed. "I knew it! I saw your face when you looked at the letters first—and now again! You do not choose to tell me what I have done. Very well, why don't you say so at once? You treat me as if I were a baby!"

Her cheeks were flushed, her mouth quivered, she looked childishly ready to cry.

"You do not choose to tell me what I have done." No, why should he? The one thing he saw clearly was that the mischief was irreparable; the less said about it, therefore, the better. There was but one avenue to fortune and love for him, and it was closed before his eyes by this night's revelation. Some men would have set to work at once to make another, but not Reynold Harding. He simply accepted the decree of Fate, and felt that he had half expected it all the time. And after all, what *had* Barbara done? Most likely he would have failed, even if his letter had been duly sent. His ill-luck would have dogged him on his way to wealth. Perhaps it was more merciful, when, with one sharp stroke, it spared him the long struggle. What right had he to find fault with Barbara, the timid messenger of misfortune? Was he to answer her brutally—"You have ruined me!"—and throw the weight of his failure on the little throbbing heart which had never been so burdened before? The very idea was absurd. It was absurd to look back, absurd to murmur; the dream of Mitchelhurst was over and done with, it was not worth a withered leaf. Let it lie where it had fallen.

"Miss Strange," he said, "I assure you you are making too much of this accident. Regrets are wasted on it. Mine was a business letter, it is true, but the chances are that it would have come to nothing. I hesitated a long while before I wrote it, and I am not sure it was not a mistake. Think no more about it."

"Will you write again?" she persisted.

"Oh, we shall see. I'm going up to town to-morrow—I can settle everything then. I don't think there will be any occasion to write."

He realised his utter severance from all his hopes when he heard himself say that he was going back to town. The girl who stood questioning him had kindled a strange brightness in his life, a light which revealed her own ripe-lipped, radiant face, and then with capricious breath had blown it out again, and left him in darkness and alone. He had lost her, and yet, by a fantastic contradiction, she had never been half so near to him as at that moment. "You are deceiving me!" she said, sorrowfully. "Don't think I don't know it! Oh, if there were anything I could do to make amends " And in her pain and pity, and her certainty that in some unspoken way she had wronged him more than she could understand, she unconsciously swayed towards Reynold with her eyes and lips uplifted. She wanted to quiet the aching of her regret. She wanted a channel through which her over-wrought feelings, might pour in atoning self-sacrifice.

He knew that she did not love him, though she herself was ignorant of her own heart, but he also knew that he might have her in his arms if he chose, acquiescent, remorseful, submissive, with her head upon his breast. That one moment was his. Through the fierce throbbing of his pulses he was oddly conscious of all his surroundings—the little room which smelt of paraffin and of unused furniture, the letters lying on the magenta table-cloth, the slippery little horse-hair sofa from which Barbara had risen to meet him; everything was mean, dreary, and hideous. But he had only to make one step across the patchwork rug of red and black, only to ask her to share that hopeless future of his, and he might take her to himself in her pliant grace, and his lips would meet hers!

He was her master, yet he stood still drawing his breath deeply, and eyeing the parti-coloured rug as if it were a yawning gulf between them. He would not cross it, he would say no word of love or of reproach to spoil her after-life, but his soul was bitter as gall. At that moment he felt himself strong enough to give up everything, but he could not be tender. Was she in later days to remember him vaguely as a poor sullen fellow whose schemes and talk came to nothing, who was too helpless to make his way in the world? Was she, perhaps, to try to do something for him—to recommend him, for instance, to some friend who wanted a tutor for a dull boy? Was she to give him her little dole of pity and friendship? No, by Heaven! he would not have that, when he might have taken herself. Why should he suffer in silence, and not inflict one answering touch of pain, if only that he might feel his power to wound? She was trying him too cruelly with that innocent offer of atonement, which meant so much more than she understood.

Because he would not speak the "Marry me, Barbara!" which was at his very lips, he controlled his voice and asked with an air of polite inquiry, "What is it that you so kindly wish to do for me?"

"What? Oh, I don't know!" she faltered in confusion. "What *can* I do? I don't know. Only if there were anything—if there ever could be——"

He looked at her, gravely at first, then with a smile that deepened slowly. She met his glance with her appealing eyes, but she could not meet his smile. Its derision reached her like a stinging lash, and she shrank away. "I *wish* I had never come!" she said in a low tone. All her sweet compassionate longing was driven back upon her heart by his mocking smile, and turned to something that choked her. "I wish I hadn't!" she repeated in a stifled voice, and went towards the door, eager to escape.

Reynold perceived that he had succeeded admirably. It seemed unlikely that Barbara would ever come to him again.

A sudden roar of wind in the chimney startled them both, and recalled him to some consciousness of the outer world. He took his hat from the table, and held the door for her to pass.

"Good-bye," she panted, still with her eyes averted.

"I'm coming with you."

"No, you are not!"

"Pardon me, but I think I am."

"No!" Barbara repeated. He smiled, but followed her. She turned on the stairs in angry helplessness and faced him. "But I would rather you didn't!" she exclaimed.

"Did you come alone?"

"Yes, and I can go back alone."

"But Mr. Hayes—what did he say?"

"He is out, he didn't know. Oh!" with a terrified glance, "if he should be back first!"

Harding unlatched the outer door, and she flew out into the rushing wind. He was at her side in a moment. "Take my arm," he said.

"I won't!" cried the girl, angrily. "Why don't you leave me when I ask you?"

"Because you can't go all through Mitchelhurst alone this stormy night—and so late," said Reynold, raising his voice to dominate an especially furious gust.

Barbara caught at Mrs. Simmonds's railings to steady herself. "Thank you!" she shouted, "it's very kind of you to remind me that I ought not to be here at this time of night!" She felt as if her words were torn out of her mouth and whirled away. She ended with something that sounded like a sob, but she herself hardly knew what it was, or what became of it.

"Nonsense!" said Reynold, as if he were hailing her from an almost hopeless distance. "You *must* let me see you safely to the gate." The gust subsided a little. "You must indeed," he added in a more natural tone.

"Will you leave me?" she persisted. "It's all I ask you!"

"Very well," he answered, angrily. "But I suppose Mitchelhurst Street is as free to me as to you, and I don't see that you can want more than half of it. Take whichever side you please, and I'll go the other."

"Good night," she said, ignoring this declaration. He waited only to ascertain her intention, and then strode across the way to the further path.

They walked through the village in this fashion, two dusky shapes, grotesquely blown and hustled by the strong wind. A capricious blast, catching Barbara's dress, would send her scudding helplessly for a few yards before she could regain her self-control. The tall figure on the other side of the road, clutching at his hat, would quicken his long steps to keep up with her involuntary increase of speed. When she contrived to pull herself up he slackened his pace, timing his movements with shadow-like accuracy and persistence.

The clouds were flying in such quick succession that for some time there was no decided break through which the moon might show her face. The heavens were a vast moving canopy, glimmering with diffused light, that grew to spectral whiteness now and again, when the veil was thin over the hidden orb. Harding blessed the obscurity which might save Miss Strange from the wondering comments of Mitchelhurst. They only met three or four men, fighting their homeward way against the wind, and, country fashion, keeping the centre of the road. One of these caught sight of Reynold, and, staring at him, shouted a jovial "Good night," to which the young man, glad to monopolise his attention, made a courteous reply, while the slim little figure, on the other side of the way, stole along in the shadow of the houses unobserved. Presently they passed beyond the village street and turned into the road which led up to the Place, where the high banks sheltered them a little, and they did not meet the wind so directly. Barbara kept to the hedgerow on the left, Reynold skirted that on the right, and though the narrower way enforced a rather closer companionship, they walked with an air of indifference as serene as the stormy night permitted.

When they reached the little slope at the gate, Harding halted. Barbara had to cross the road, and while she did so he stood perfectly still, not attempting to lessen the distance between them by one step. The wild noise of the blast in the tree tops made a kind of rushing accompaniment to the silence. All at once the ragged clouds parted, and the moon sailed suddenly into a blue rift. Everything became coldly and brilliantly distinct, even to the lock of the wrought-iron gate, towards which Barbara stretched an ungloved hand. As she touched it she hesitated.

"Mr. Harding," she said.

There was a lull between two gusts, and the fury which had preceded it made it seem like an absolute and charmed tranquillity. Reynold advanced at her summons with a slightly exaggerated obedience. The moon was at his back and his black shadow seemed to hurry before him, to throw itself at the girl's feet, and then to slip past her through the iron bars, as if it would creep into Mitchelhurst Place, and take possession by stealth.

"Why did you make me angry?" said Barbara in a tremulous voice. "Why did we come through the village in this idiotic way?"

"I was under the impression that you declined my escort," he replied, with conscious meekness.

"You make me behave rudely—*why* do you? I went to your lodgings to tell you how sorry I was, and to ask your pardon for my carelessness, and it seems as if I went for nothing but to quarrel. Any one would think so. Perhaps you think so?"

"No," said Reynold, smiling, "I don't. And it isn't a very serious quarrel, is it?"

"Don't sneer at me any more, or you will make me hateful!" cried Barbara. "I can't bear it! I will never ask you again if there is anything I can do—never! You needn't have shown me how you despised me: you might have been a little kinder when I went to you like that!"

She swallowed down a sob.

"Really I'm very sorry if anything I said—" he began.

"Oh never mind now what you said or did! I know it, and that's enough. I won't give you another chance, but I won't quarrel. It hurts me, it's horrid, it's worse than Uncle Hayes. Do let us part friends—or—or—something like friends— not in this miserable way!"

"With all my heart."

She took her hand from the gate and turned towards him.

"Say you forgive me then! For everything!"

"Ah! that I can't do," Reynold replied, finding a kind of distorted pleasure in playing with her earnestness. "I'm not sure, yet, that there is anything to forgive."

"Forgive me on the chance!"

"Oh no, I couldn't presume to do that! It would be a chance whether *you* forgave *me* afterwards for my impertinence."

A sudden blast nearly sent her tottering into his arms. She recovered herself, looked at him in speechless indignation as if he had ordered it, pushed open the gate, and the black tracery of bars swung back into its place, dividing them.

Reynold stood where she had left him, gazing after her. She went a little way up the drive, and then lingered, half turning as if she thought some one had called. The ground on which she stood was dry and white in the moonshine, and dappled with fantastic, moving shadows. The little old trees fought against the wind, swaying their bare, misshapen arms above her head. The stone balls on either side of the entrance gleamed like skulls in the pale light, guarding the avenue to the sepulchral house, with its glassy rows of windows. For a moment the picture was as clear as day, with Barbara standing in the middle of the road; then a great wave of stormy cloud rolled up and overtopped the moon, and in the dusky confusion she vanished.

CHAPTER IV.
REYNOLD'S REGRET.

With the passing of that gleam of moonlight it seemed to Reynold Harding that Mitchelhurst Place disappeared finally into the abyss that waits for all created things. Where the house, in its curious ghastly whiteness, had stood a moment earlier, was now nothing but baffling gloom, and the very gate vanished into the shadows, as if there were no need of any substantial barrier between him and the lost vision. The scene had closed with dramatic suddenness, and he felt that the play was played out, but how long he stood staring at the dusky curtain he did not know.

At last he turned, and made his way down the dim road. The bewildering obscurity seemed to press upon his sight, and he quickened his pace to gain the corner where his glance might rest on the scattered lamps of Mitchelhurst Street—little flames shuddering and struggling in the gale. He had gone about half the distance to his lodgings, when he saw two advancing eyes of fire at the end of the street. Nearer and nearer they came, but, owing to the clamour of the wind, the noise of wheels was inaudible till the carriage was close upon him where he paused on the sidewalk. Then for a moment there was a gleam of light upon the road, and in it appeared, as in a kind of magic-lantern picture, a sorry-looking grey horse, travelling reluctantly beyond his stable at the inn, a shabby driver, buttoned closely against the wind, with his hat pulled low on his brows, a flashing of revolving wheels, and the black silhouette of the Mitchelhurst fly. Harding looked after it till he saw the lamp shine for a moment, with sudden brightness, as the carriage turned, and then go out. After this fashion was Mr. Hayes, too, lost in the darkness which had swallowed everything else, and Reynold's gaze conveyed a not unkindly farewell.

The night gathered and deepened in the village, and the great starless dome bent its vaulted gloom over the half-dozen lights which glimmered on cottages and cabbage plots. Now and again a dog would bark, or the wind would pass with a wilder wail, and the sign of the *Rothwell Arms* would creak discordantly. The people to whom that little hollow was the world, lay close and safe in their houses, wakened, perhaps, by the gale to hope that no tiles would fall, and no damage be done in the gardens, listening drowsily for awhile, and then turning in their beds to sleep again.

It was not till the moon was low in the west that it broke once more through the clouds, and, peering in at a small uncurtained window, revealed the white face of a man who sat by it, with drooping head and listless hands. He was not asleep, but he did not move. With that same glance the moon espied St. Michael in the lancet window, sedulously trampling on his little dragon, while the old clock above his head recorded the passing of the hours with a labour of slow strokes. Those two, and those two only, did the moon see in all Mitchelhurst, and then vanished again and left them, till the wind went down, and the day came slowly over the grey fields, with a deluge of autumnal rain.

Mrs. Simmonds was sorry to lose her lodger, and sorry that the weather should be so bad, and that he should look so pale. She busied herself about his breakfast, and brought him the local paper with the air of a successful prophet.

"I told you there'd be another to-day, sir," she said as she laid it down, "and here it is!" Reynold briefly acknowledged the attention, but he never touched it. "So set as he was upon that other one!" said Mrs. Simmonds later to her husband.

Simmonds suggested that he might have found something that specially interested him in the other paper, somebody dead and leaving money, may be, or somebody mysteriously disappeared, or something—he looked as if he'd had a shock of some sort. But Mrs. Simmonds was inclined to think that he was most likely upset by the thought of his railway journey. She knew it was all *she* could do to swallow a bit, if she were going anywhere, with all her packing on her mind, and very likely the gentleman was of the same way of feeling. As to a shock, he hadn't got any shock out of the paper, she knew. He might have had some bad news in the letters Miss Strange brought him, for he told her with his own lips that they were very important, and that was why she came with them herself.

"You see, the old gentleman was out," said Mrs. Simmonds, "so I suppose she didn't know what to do."

"I shouldn't think the old gentleman would be best pleased," said Simmonds.

The good woman considered for a moment.

"Well, I sha'n't tell him," she announced finally.

Harding drove to the nearest station in a gig. The rain was not so heavy then, the downpour had become a persistent drizzle. Nevertheless the village looked drenched and dismal enough as he bade it good-bye, and swung round the corner of the churchyard wall, where the yellow weeds stood up in the crevices behind the slant grey veil, and the great black-plumaged yews let fall their heavy tears upon the graves. In another minute a clump of trees hid the square tower and the leaden roof, and Mitchelhurst was left behind. But the young man looked right and left at the wet hedgerows till they reached a spot where a ploughed field rose above the bank on one side, while on the other a deep bramble-grown ditch divided the road from the sodden meadows. He fixed his eyes on that. It was exactly a week that Wednesday since he first met Barbara Strange.

Late that afternoon he walked into a dull room in a dull suburb of London, and a woman who stood in the window, snipping the dead fronds from a homesick-looking fern, turned to meet him. There was no mistaking the relationship. Allowing for the differences of sex and age, they were as like as they could possibly be, except that in every glance and gesture the woman showed a fuller and richer life than did the man. There was something of imperious grace in her movements which made him seem awkward, hesitating, and constrained. She suffered him to touch her cheek with his lips, but showed no inclination to speak first.

"Back again, you see," he said, drawing a chair to the hearth-rug.

"Yes. I should think you must be wet."

"Damp, I suppose."

He glanced round the room. The flock paper, the red curtains, the grimy windows, the smoky fire, had the strange novelty which the most familiar things will sometimes put on. The atmosphere was loaded with acrid fog, and the blackness of the great city. He raised his foot and warmed a muddy boot, while his thoughts went back to the stateliness and airy purity of the old manor house, where the great logs cracked and glowed upon the hearths.

Mrs. Harding came and rested her elbow on the chimney-piece, looking down at her son.

"I left Mitchelhurst this morning," said he, after a pause.

"Yes? Well, I suppose you had seen enough of it."

"It was time to come home, anyhow," he said.

"You had business in town?"

The tone and words would have served as well for any chance visitor.

"Yes—naturally."

He put the other foot to the fire by way of a change.

"I did not know," said Mrs. Harding. "I have nothing to do with your business. It certainly isn't mine. You are always welcome to be here as much as you please, but of course you will attend to your own affairs."

31

Reynold made no answer.

"You are your own master," she continued, after a short silence. "I have recognised that for some years. I have not expected you to go my way."

"One must go one's own way, I suppose," said the young man.

"And if I expected you to show some slight consideration for me, in taking the way you have chosen—I was mistaken!"

He stirred the fire, and replaced the poker, but did not look at her or speak.

"You know what I mean?" she demanded.

"Perfectly."

"Reynold, you might have written! Your uncle's offer deserved a word. I do not say you might have accepted it, but you might have refused it courteously. Was that so much to ask? You have insulted him wantonly, and he will never pardon it. After all, he is your father's brother, and an old man. Reynold, you should have written!"

He did not raise his eyes from the burning coals.

"Well," he said, "I did propose to write before I went away."

She winced at the thrust.

"I was wrong!" she owned, with bitter passion in her voice. "It would have been better."

"As things have turned out," said Reynold, "I think it would."

Poor little Barbara! If that angry, dark-eyed woman had known how near the fulfilment of her hopes had been, and lost by how pitiful a chance? But the secret was safe.

Kate Harding drew a long breath.

"Well, I have no more to say about it. Perhaps it is best that we should understand each other. You knew how your silence would wound me; it was deliberate—it was calculated. Well, it *has* wounded me, I don't deny it. But it is all over now, and you will never wound me again. Do what you please, now and always—as you have done."

He signified his attention sullenly, with a slight movement of his head.

"It is all over," she continued. "The situation is filled up, and nothing would ever induce Robert Harding to suffer you to enter his office—not if you offered to sweep it! He will not trouble you any more, and, since the matter is ended, let it never be mentioned between us again."

It was easy to see that she was, as she had said, deeply wounded, and there was a tragical intensity in her speech. Her son made answer with the same mute gesture of assent.

Presently she moved away, and for a few minutes she busied herself about the room. She gathered up the leaves she had cut off, put away two or three things that were lying about, and then came back to him.

"Dinner will be ready at the usual time," she said, in a cold, everyday voice. "And then we can talk——of other things."

"Yes," Reynold answered, with a start, looking up from his reverie. He had been thinking of the evening before. When he went into the little sitting-room after his walk, and Barbara rose up from the sofa to meet him, he had been startled, she was confused and frightened, and they had forgotten the ordinary greetings. And then they had talked, he had sat looking at her, he had stood up and held himself aloof—*how* had he done it? Well, it had been for Barbara's sake. Afterwards they had gone through Mitchelhurst together. Together? No, absurdly apart, with the breadth of the street between them. And at last they had talked at the gate, and he had vexed her, and she had hurried away without a word of farewell. It seemed to him now that he had never meant that. It was impossible he could have meant it. Why, they had never shaken hands, he had never touched her, and he remembered that she had no glove on, he had seen her hand in the moonlight on the latch of the gate. She had said, "Let us part friends," he had only to consent.

It is well that we cannot recall our moments of temptation. Reynold had been able to pain her then with a jest, he had been strong enough in his bitterness of heart to let her go without a word, but now as he sat staring at the fire, idly clasping his knee, he regretted his strength. If he could have taken Barbara's hand he would, and the long fingers, loosely knit together, suddenly tightened at the thought. A woman's small hand would not have had much chance of escape from such a clasp as that.

But at that moment his mother aroused him from his musings.

CHAPTER V.
LOVE'S MESSENGER.

The first week of December had not gone by, and already the winter had set in. Mr. Pryor, as he walked from the vicarage up the lonely road to Mitchelhurst Place, said to himself that it was a most unpleasant afternoon. Of his own free will he would not have left his fireside, but Destiny had turned him out, and he went feebly and heavily along the iron road, feeling as if Nature were in a mood of freezing malice and took pleasure in his sufferings. The air was still, yet it came very keenly to his pallid face, his feet were cold, the hand that held his umbrella was remarkably cold, a red-edged manual of prayers and devotional readings, tucked under his left arm, showed a tendency to slip, and altogether Mr. Pryor had a half-numbed sense that it was not fair that any one should want him in such weather.

The sky was grey, a chilly fog narrowed the horizon, and all the hedges and boughs in the little frozen landscape were covered with hoarfrost. It was like a dream of a dead spring. Every little clump of trees was an orchard, white with sterile blossoming, spectral flowers which would vanish as suddenly as they had come. Every sound was deadened, till it was almost startling to come upon a man at work by the wayside, lopping hoary branches from the hedge, and flinging them down, with all their delicate tangle of white sprays, upon the frosted grass. It was a grim task to be the only sign of energy in that ghostlike world; such a task as in an old picture Death himself might have undertaken. Happily, however, for good Mr. Pryor's nerves, it was the face of an ordinary flesh and blood labourer, with the breath steaming from his gaping mouth, that was lifted as he went by.

The vicar crept, shivering, up the avenue to the house, which was more than ever like a great white tomb. He asked the servant who admitted him how Mr. Hayes was that afternoon.

"Much the same, thank you, sir," said the woman, showing him into the yellow drawing-room, and putting a piece of wood on the fire, "I'll tell Miss Strange you are here."

He stood miserably on the rug, looking down into the fender, and squeezing his red-edged book under his arm, till at the sound of the opening door he turned and saw Barbara. The girl came forward quickly, and touched the fumbling fingers which he held out, as she uttered a word of greeting.

"Mr. Hayes is much the same, they tell me," said the clergyman in a melancholy voice.

"Yes," said Barbara, "I suppose there isn't any difference. But I think anyhow he isn't any worse. Mamma is with him, and he was taking some beef-tea just now"—Mr. Pryor nodded grave approval of the beef-tea—"but he'll be very glad to see you in a few minutes. Won't you sit down?"

He sat down, nursing the book, which had a narrow ribbon hanging out of it.

"I hope Mrs. Strange is pretty well—as well as can be expected?" he said, after a pause. "Not over-fatigued, I trust?"

"Oh, no; I don't think so," the girl replied. "Mamma seems very well."

"Ah, quite so. She bears up, she bears up. Well, that is what we must all try to do—to bear up. It is the only thing."

"Yes," said Barbara. She was not quite sure that she ought to have said that her mother seemed very well. "Of course it is a trying time," she added, by way of softening the possibly indiscreet admission.

"Certainly, certainly—very trying for you both," Mr. Pryor agreed. Yet even to his dull eyes it was apparent that this very trying time had not dimmed the bright face opposite. There was a peculiar radiance and warmth of youth about Barbara that afternoon, a glow of life which forced itself on his perception. She did not smile, she was very quiet, and yet it seemed as if some new delight, some unspoken hope, had awakened within her, quickening and kindling her to the very finger-tips. She sat demurely in her low chair, with her face turned towards the window, but there was a soft flame of colour on her cheek, and a light in her eyes when she lifted her drooping lashes. In that great, cold house, through which the shadow of death was creeping, she was the incarnation of life and promise, a curious contrast to her surroundings. It would hardly have seemed stranger if suddenly, in the desolate world without, one had come on a burning bush of pomegranate flowers among the cold frost-blossoms of the Mitchelhurst hedges.

Mr. Pryor felt something of all this. He did not quite like it. Of course he did not want to see the girl haggard and weary, but he was so chilly, as he sat there by the fireside with his book on his knee, that it seemed to him as if the swift, light pulsations of youth were hardly proper. He would have been more at his ease with Barbara if she had had a slight toothache, or a cold in her head. He felt it his duty to depress her a little, quietly, as she sat there.

"The hour of Death's approach is a very solemn one, even for the bystanders," Mr. Pryor began, after a moment's consideration.

Barbara said, "Yes it was," with an almost disconcerting readiness.

"Yes, yes, and we should endeavour to profit by it. We should spend it, not only in regrets for those who are about to be taken from us, but in thoughts of the future."

Barbara's red lips parted in another "Yes." The future—she was thinking of it. It was easier to think of it than of the old man who was dying.

"Of the future," Mr. Pryor continued, caressing the smooth leather of his book with his ungloved hand, and softly pulling the pendent ribbon, "of the time when we shall be lying—yes, yes, each one of us—as our friend is now." He glanced up at the ceiling, to indicate that he meant Mr. Hayes, taking his beef-tea in the bed-room on the first floor.

The girl said nothing, but looked meditatively at the folds of her dress, as if she were in church. It would have been pleasanter if Mr. Pryor had brought a funeral sermon out of his table drawer, and could have gone on without these embarrassing pauses.

"When our hour is at hand," he said at last, "as—as it must be one of these days. How shall we feel then, Miss Strange?"

Barbara didn't know.

"No," said the vicar, "we don't know. But we must think—we must think. Try to picture yourself in your uncle's position—what would your life look to you if you were lying there now?"

She looked up with a sudden startled flash. "I haven't had my life—it would only look like a beginning," she said with a vision as of a rose-garlanded doorway to a vault. "If I were going to die directly I couldn't feel like Uncle Hayes."

The passionate speech awoke the clergyman's instinct of assent. "No, no," he said, "certainly not. Certainly not." At that moment a message came: "Would Mr. Pryor kindly step up-stairs?" and he went, not altogether sorry to bring his little discourse to a close.

Barbara, left to herself, sat gazing at the window, till at last the hinted smile, which had troubled her companion, betrayed itself in a tender, changeful curve. "Adrian!" she said softly, under her breath. "Oh, how could I? How could I? Adrian! and I thought you didn't care!"

She was restless with happiness. She sprang up, and walked to and fro, too glad at heart to complain of the walls that held her, and yet feeling that she needed air and freedom for her joy. She leaned against the window, and looked out at the wintry world, murmuring Adrian's name against the chilly pane. There was no voice to give her back her tender speech, yet she hardly missed it. No praise is so sweet to a woman as the reproaches she heaps upon herself for an unjust suspicion of her lover. To defend him to others is a mixture of joy and pain, but to feel that she has wronged him, and that to trust him is safer than to trust her doubts, is a passionate delight.

This joy had come to Barbara that very morning. She had been sitting in her uncle's room, reading a novel by the fireside, while the old man slept, as she thought. She softly turned page after page till a feeble voice broke the silence. "Where's your mamma?" said Mr. Hayes.

"Down-stairs, writing letters. Do you want her?" And Barbara stood ready to go.

"No, I don't want her. Writing her daily bulletins, eh? Well, well. What's the time? You haven't given me my medicine."

"It's very nearly time," said Barbara, with a glance at the clock. There was a little clinking of bottle and glass, and then she came to the bedside, and stood looking down at the wrinkled, fallen face among the pillows. "Can I help you?" she asked.

"Wait a bit, can't you?" said the old man.

She waited, looking aside, yet watching for the slightest movement on his part. Her soft young fingers closed round the half-filled glass, and his dim eyes rested on them. Presently he raised himself with an effort, and the girl put another pillow behind him. He stretched out a trembling, dingy-white hand, carried the glass to his lips a little uncertainly, and emptied it.

She set it down. "Shall I take away that pillow?" she asked.

"No—wait."

Barbara, after a minute, shifted her position, and stood by the carved post at the foot of the bed, while her thoughts went back to her novel. She was not heartless, she was only young. Her uncle had never been very much to her, and she found it as difficult to concentrate her mind on this melancholy business of sickness and dissolution as if it were a sermon. And yet she did sincerely desire to behave properly, and to feel properly, too, if it could be managed.

The little old man rested awhile, sitting up in his bed. He perceived that the girl's thoughts were far away. He could keep her standing there as long as he pleased, a motionless figure against the faded green curtains, but he could not narrow her world to his sick-room. Perhaps for that very reason he felt a desire to awaken her from her reverie.

"How old are you?" he asked.

"Nineteen."

The answer was given with a lifting of her long lashes. She had not expected any question about herself.

"Nineteen?"

"Yes. At least I shall be nineteen next month."

A month more or less made little difference to Barbara.

"As much as that?" he said. "Barbara, perhaps I ought to say something before I go."

Her attention was effectually aroused, and her brilliant gaze rested on the dull, waxen mask before her. But after a moment his eyes fell away from hers.

"I thought I did right," he said.

"Yes?" Barbara questioned.

"That young man who came here—what was his name?"

"Mr. Harding."

"No, no, no!" he cried irritably. "No! What made you think of him? The first one?"

"Mr. Scarlett?"

He nodded.

"But it doesn't matter," he said. "If you were thinking of the other one it doesn't matter about Scarlett."

"What about him?"

"He wanted to speak to you before he went away, and I told him to wait. Better to wait—you were so young, you know."

"He *did* want to speak to me!" the girl exclaimed under her breath.

"Plenty of time," said Mr. Hayes. "He's young too. I told him he could come again to Mitchelhurst if he felt the same. I thought it was best—I thought it was best," he repeated, trying to drown a faint consciousness that to have parted with Barbara would have upset all his arrangements.

"I'm sure you did," she answered soothingly.

"I know your mother would say it was best—wouldn't she? Besides, I didn't do any harm, since you were thinking of the other one."

"He was here last," said Barbara.

"So he was," the sick man answered, with a flash of his old briskness. "And girls soon forget."

Barbara said nothing. What was the good of protestations? She would never utter a word against Reynold Harding—never. And what could she say about Adrian Scarlett? She had not owned to herself that she cared for him. If she did—and she was conscious of strong pulsations, which flushed her face, and filled her veins with tingling warmth—the more reason for silence. She laid a hand on the carved foliage of the post, and faced the dim figure propped in the bed. There was something grotesquely feeble about the little man's attitude. His face, discoloured and pale, drooped in the greenish shadow of the hangings, his unshaven chin rested on his breast, his parchment hands lay in a little nerveless heap on the counterpane before him. One would have said that he was set up in sport, as children set up dolls and nine-pins, on purpose to be knocked over.

"Hadn't you better lie down?" said Barbara, after considering him for a while. She wanted to speak tenderly, for the sake of the strange new gladness which was throbbing at her heart; yet the facts of sickness and hopeless decay had never seemed so distasteful. When he assented, she put her arm about him with the utmost care, but she could hardly help shrinking from the clutch of his chilly fingers on her wrist.

"Rothwells are a bad lot," he said, "bad and poor. Scarlett would be a better match. Some of his people have money."

The habit of deference to her Uncle Hayes prevented her from resenting this speech.

"Never mind about that, please, uncle," she said gently.

"Good family, too," said Mr. Hayes, indistinctly to himself. "I did it for the best, as your mamma would see."

"Never mind about mamma, Uncle Hayes," said the girl again. "I'm sure you had better rest a little."

And when he acquiesced she went back to her novel, which was all about Adrian Scarlett. After all, he had not gone off without a thought of her—he had *not* slighted her. Perhaps she was too young, and at any rate she could not be angry with her uncle since he had told her of Adrian's love. She had a right to think of him as Adrian, surely, if he loved her. So he had been sent away— where? Perhaps he would see somebody else, somebody better and more beautiful, and she would be forgotten. Well!—Barbara's eyes were fixed intently on the page—even if he did forget her, it might break her heart, but she need not be ashamed that she had thought of him, since she held the happy certainty that he had thought of her. Happen what might in his after life, he had loved her once—he had!—he had! And she had feared that he had only laughed at her, she had thought that he might be heartless—Oh how was it possible that she could have been so wickedly unjust! She deserved that he should never come back to her.

It was an incongruous business altogether. It was as if a breath from a burial vault had quickened the faint flame in Barbara's heart to sudden splendour, for if old Hayes had actually been the mummy he very much resembled, he could not have been more remote from any comprehension of the message which he had delivered. His lips had relaxed in utter feebleness, and the secret had escaped. He did not see the look which flashed into the girl's eyes, and when Mrs. Strange, who might have been more observant, came to take her place by the bedside, Barbara stole softly away, hanging her head in the consciousness of those flushed cheeks, which seemed too like holiday wear for such a melancholy time. Her mother might have been surprised, for she had been a little uneasy, fancying that the girl looked sad. Barbara was but a young thing, and had been left too long shut up with but dismal company.

And, if Mrs. Strange had only known it, the poor little girl had been her own most dismal company. From the time that Reynold Harding went away she had been restless, frightened, and miserable. When the exaltation of that evening had passed, a sudden terror at the thought of her own daring overtook her. She was not only afraid of her uncle's anger, but doubtful whether she had not really committed an unpardonable sin against the social law. When she hurried to Harding with the letters, she had somehow vaguely believed that he would shelter her, that he would stand by her if she were blamed. And when he had played with her, refused to trust her, and vanished into the night with a mocking smile, leaving her utterly alone, she had felt absurdly desolate. At first she had waited, in sickening apprehension, for her uncle to hear of her visit to Mr. Harding. Fate, however, seemed whimsically inclined to protect her. First there was the storm of rain which prevented a meeting with all the gossips of Mitchelhurst at the Penny Reading. Then, a day or two later, came Mr. Hayes' accident—a mere slip on the stairs, it was supposed, till the doctor hinted at something in the nature of a fit. Barbara saw that detection was postponed, but still she felt that the sword hung over her head, and night after night she tossed in an agony of doubt. Had she really done anything very dreadful? She recalled Mr. Harding's ambiguous words and glances—did they mean that he thought lightly of a girl who would go to him as she had done? Over and over again she asked the useless questions—Did they mean that?—Did they not?—What *did* they mean? And leaving his meaning out of the matter, what would other people say? Suppose she went and told them—ah! but how and what would she tell them? She might say, "I found I hadn't posted Mr. Harding's letters, so I took them to him at once: wasn't that the best thing to do?" How right and reasonable it sounded! But if she said, "I went secretly to a man's lodgings at night——" at the mere thought a blush passed over her like a scorching wave of fire. What would her mother say?

Even in her misery she was childish enough to wince at the thought of her sisters at home. She had been proud to be mistress of a house while they were still in the school-room, and the idea that she had been wanting in dignity, perhaps even in modesty, and that she might be ostentatiously controlled and watched, by way of punishment, was intolerable to her. To be humiliated before Louisa and Hetty—how could she endure it? They were not ill- natured, but they had a little resented her advancement, and Barbara, as she lay in her great over-shadowing bed, could fancy all the out-spoken comments and questionings in the roomy attic where the three used to sleep. She did not want to go back to the Devonshire vicarage, and yet Mitchelhurst was fast becoming hateful to her. The pictures on the walls gazed at her with Reynold's eyes, his presence haunted the house from which he had been banished. What was the wrong that she had done him? She did not know, and the uncertainty seemed to mock her as he had mocked her that night. The poor child said to herself quite seriously that he had taken away all her youth and happiness. She fancied that she felt old and weary as the days went by, fretting her simple heart with unacknowledged fear.

And now suddenly came the message of Adrian's love, and lifted her above all her dreary little troubles. What did it matter that it was uttered by those dry, bloodless lips, which stumbled over the blissful words? What did anything matter since Adrian cared for her, and life was all to come? Why had she tormented herself about Reynold Harding! *Reynold Harding!* He was utterly insignificant, he was nobody! She could tell Adrian about that expedition of hers, it was so unimportant, so trivial, that he could not be jealous; he could not mind. Adrian's jealousy! There was something delightful, even in that terrible possibility. But he would not be jealous, everything was warm, and glad, and full of sunshine when Adrian was there.

She resented Mr. Pryor's professional allusions to the uncertainty of life. There are moments so perfect that they ought not to be degraded by thoughts of disease and death, ought not to be measured or weighed in any way whatever. Barbara felt this, and she thrust aside the clergyman's lecture as soon as he left the room. Let him talk of such things to Uncle Hayes. As for her, she lingered at the window, thinking of her newly-found happiness, while she gazed at the hoary fields, with their black boundaries of railing or leafless hedge, till a faint pink flush crept over the pale sky, as if it were softly suffused with her overflowing joy. Mitchelhurst Place, of which Harding had dreamed so tenderly a few months earlier, as a home for himself and his love, was to the eager girl at that moment only a charnel-house, full of death and clinging memories, from which she panted to escape. It was true that she had first met Adrian Scarlett there, but she had the whole world in which to meet him again. "And he will always know where to find me," she said to herself with a touch of practical common sense in the midst of her rapture. "He can look out papa's name in the Clergy List, any day."

CHAPTER VI.
A PERPLEXING REFLECTION.

The April sun was shining into two pleasant sitting-rooms, only divided by a partially drawn curtain. Their long windows opened on a wide gravel walk. Beyond this lay a garden, bright with the airy, leafless charm of spring. The grass was grey-green as yet, the borders brown earth, but there were lines and patches of gay spring flowers, and a blithe activity of birds, while the white clouds floated far away in the breezy sky.

Adrian Scarlett, who was a guest in the house, came slowly sauntering along one of the sunshiny paths, between the yellow daffodils, with eyes intent on a handful of printed leaves. Now and again he stopped short, trying a different reading of a line, or twisting his little pointed beard with white fingers, while he questioned some doubtful harmony of syllables. Once he took a pencil from his pocket, and with indignant amusement marked a misprint. After each of these pauses he resumed his dreamy progress, unconscious of any wider horizon than the margin of his page.

Presently his loitering walk brought him to one of the tall, shining windows, and thrusting the little bundle of proofs into his pocket, he unfastened it and stepped in. He found the room untenanted, except by two or three flies, which buzzed in the sunny panes as if summer time had come. A piano stood open, with some music lying on it, and the young man sat down with his back to the curtained opening, began to play, and amused himself for a while in an agreeably discursive fashion. But after a time he felt that he was not alone. The conviction stole upon him gradually, though, as far as he knew, there had been no sound in the further room, and he had previously believed that everybody was out. He glanced over his shoulder more than once, but saw nothing.

"Shall I go and look?" he asked himself. "But it may be somebody I don't know, and don't want to know. Suppose it should be a housemaid come to be hired, and waiting till Mrs. Wilton comes in. What should I say to the housemaid? Or, by the way, the parson said something about Easter offerings yesterday, perhaps this is the clerk or somebody come for them. Perhaps if I go in he'll ask me for an Easter offering. I think I won't risk it. Shall I go into the garden again?"

While he debated the question, he went on playing, feeling that the music justified an apparent unconsciousness of the invisible companionship. The sunshine lighted up the reddish golden tint of his hair and moustache, and the warm flesh colours of his face. Presently his wandering fingers slackened on the keys, and then after a momentary pause of recollection he struck the first notes of a simple air, and played it, with his head thrown back and a smile on his lips.

Near him an old-fashioned mirror hung, a little slanted, on the wall, and as his roving eyes fell on it, a beardless, sharply-cut face appeared in its shadows, motionless and pale, gazing out of the heavy frame with a singular look of eagerness.

Adrian started, but his surprise was so quickly mastered that it was hardly perceptible, and he continued as if nothing had happened, apparently suffering his glances to wander as before, though in reality he watched the dark eyes and sullen brows bent on him from the wall. The face appearing so picturesquely, interested him, and after a moment the interest deepened. As he had before become gradually conscious of the man's presence, so now did a certainty steal over him that he was somehow familiar with the features in the mirror.

The stranger was evidently standing where he might see and not be seen, and he leant on a high-backed chair so that he was partially hidden.

"Who the deuce is he? and where have I seen him? and what does he want here?" said Scarlett to himself, continuing to play the tune which had evoked the apparition. "He doesn't look as if he went round for Easter offerings. Can't want to tune the piano, or why didn't he begin before I came in? Hope he isn't an escaped lunatic—there's something queer and fixed about his eyes; perhaps I had better soothe him with a softer strain. By Jove! I *have* seen him somewhere, and uncommonly good-looking he is, too! How can I have forgotten him? He isn't the sort of man to forget. He doesn't look quite modern, somehow, with his full, dark hair, and his beardless face; or, rather, I *feel* as if he were not quite modern—but why?"

Adrian glided into the accompaniment to an old song, and sang a quaint verse or two softly to himself. The face in the mirror relaxed a little. After a moment the man straightened himself, drew back, and vanished. Adrian finished his song, and then, in the silence that ensued, a slight movement was audible, enough to warrant his entering the further room, as if he had just suspected the presence of a visitor.

The man of the mirror was sitting in an arm-chair, with a book in his hand. He looked up a little hesitatingly and awkwardly, as if he were doubtful whether to rise or not. Adrian hastened to apologise for his musical performance.

"I had no idea there was any one here," he said. "I hope I didn't disturb you?"

"Not at all," said the stranger, glancing at the book he held, and furtively reversing it. "An enviable talent," he added, with an evident effort.

"For oneself, perhaps," answered Scarlett. "But I'm not sure it is desirable in a next-door neighbour."

He was still trying to identify his companion. The voice, unmusical and almost harsh, did not help him in the least, and, oddly enough, now that they were actually face to face, he was less absolutely certain that he ought to recognise the man. "It may be only a likeness to somebody I know," he reflected. "But to whom, then? And why does he look at me like that? *He* seems to think he knows *me*!"

"I hope you'll go on if you feel inclined," said the stranger.

Adrian shook his head.

"Thank you, but I think I've made about noise enough for one morning."

He took up the paper and skimmed a column or two. Presently he looked from behind it, and their eyes met.

"I can't help thinking," he said, "that we have met before somewhere, haven't we? I don't know where, but I have an idea that your memory is better than mine."

The other was obviously taken by surprise.

"No," he said, drawing back and frowning. "No—in fact I'm sure we haven't met—at least not to my knowledge. My name is Harding."

Scarlett owned that the name conveyed nothing to his mind, but when in return he mentioned his own, he was certain that he caught a flash of recognition in the other's eyes. "He expected that," he soliloquised, as he picked up his paper again. "Here is a mystery! Deuce take the fellow—why did he stare at me so? He isn't as handsome as I thought he was in the glass— he's ill-tempered and awkward; it isn't a pleasant face, though of course the features are good. He might make a good picture—and, by Jove! that's what he was—a picture! and I didn't know him out of his frame! I wonder whether it's a chance resemblance, or whether——"

"Were you ever at a place called Mitchelhurst?" he asked, abruptly.

The blood mounted to Harding's face.

"Yes," he said.

"Then," said Adrian, "you must surely be some connection of the family at the old Place—the *old* family at the old Place, I mean. I have made out the likeness that puzzled me. There is a picture there——"

"I am connected with the family," said Harding, "on my mother's side. It isn't much to boast of——"

"If you come to that," Scarlett answered lightly, "what is? But I'll confess—I dare say I ought to be ashamed of myself—but I'll confess that I *do* care about such things. I don't want to boast, but I would rather my ancestors were gentlemen, than that they were butchers and bakers and—well, the candlestick-makers might be decorative artists in their way, and so a trifle better."

Harding scowled, but did not speak.

"You don't agree with me," Adrian went on, with his pleasant smile. "Well, you can afford to scorn the pride of long descent if you choose. And, mind you, though I prefer the gentleman, I dare say the trades-man might be more valuable to the community at large!"

"I hope so," said Harding with a sneer. "My grandfather was a pork-butcher."

"Oh!" exclaimed Adrian, blankly. "You combine both, certainly!" He was decidedly taken aback by the announcement, as the other had intended, but he recovered himself first. It was Harding who looked sullen and ill at ease after the revelation into which he had been betrayed, as if his grandfather had somehow recoiled upon him, and knocked him down.

Young Scarlett felt that he could not get up and go away the moment the pork-butcher was introduced, though he half regretted that he had come from the piano to talk to his sulky descendant. "Well, you get your looks from your ancestors at Mitchelhurst," he said; "it's quite wonderful. I studied those portraits a good deal, and there's one on the right-hand side of the fire-place in the yellow drawing-room, as they call it—do you know the house well?"

"Yes, well enough. Yes, I know Anthony Rothwell's picture."

"It might be yours," said Adrian.

Reynold's only answer was a doubtful "Hm!"

"A fine old house!" Scarlett remarked, as he rose from his chair. If his companion intended to treat him to such curt, half-hostile speeches, he would leave him alone, and ask Mrs. Wilton, or one of the girls, about him, later. He might satisfy his curiosity so, more pleasantly.

But, "A fine old house!" Harding repeated. "Yes, a fine, dreary, chilly, decaying, melancholy old house." He leant back in his chair and looked up at Scarlett, "Did you ever see a more hopeless place in all your life?"

"Come! Not so bad as that!"

"Well, it seems to me that there is no hope about it," Reynold persisted; "no hope at all. A ghastly nightmare of a house. Why doesn't somebody pull it down!"

"You must have seen it under unfavourable circumstances."

"Very likely. I was there last October. It might be better in the summer-time."

"You stayed there?"

"Yes, a few days."

"Did they tell you I had been?" Scarlett asked, impulsively. "Did they speak of me—Mr. Hayes, and—Miss Strange?"

The men looked at each other as the name was spoken, Reynold's dark gaze crossing the bright grey-blue gleam of Adrian's glance. "They said something of a Mr. Scarlett who had been there—yes."

"And they were well, I hope?"

"Well enough—then."

"Then?" cried Adrian. "Then! Why, what has happened since?"

"Didn't you know old Hayes was dead?"

The young man drew a long breath. "No, I didn't!"

"Died just a week before Christmas. The old house is shut up."

Adrian was silent for a moment. "Poor old fellow!" he said at last. "I'm very sorry to hear it. And the house shut up—of course Miss Strange would go back to her people in Devonshire." Reynold looked at him silently. "I wonder who will take the old Place!" said Adrian. "If I were rich—" Their glances met once more, and he stopped short, and strolled towards the window.

"A castle in the air," he said, presently. "I don't suppose I shall ever see Mitchelhurst again, since the poor old gentleman is gone. But I shall always remember the place. Not for its beauty, precisely. I know when I went there first I was surprised that he should care to live in a corner of that great white pile. Something rather sepulchral about it. Did you ever notice it by moonlight?"

Reynold Harding said, Yes, he had.

"I recollect an almost startling effect one night," Scarlett continued. "And the avenue too—that queer avenue—gnarled boughs, with thin foliage quivering in the wind, and glimpses of summer sky shining through. I think if I were a painter I would make a picture of those trees."

There *was* a picture of them, stripped of their leaves, and wrestling with an October gale, before the eyes of the man to whom he spoke. "They might be worth painting," he said. "I suppose they weren't worth cutting down. If they had been, I fancy there wouldn't be any avenue left."

"I suppose not. Well, anyhow I'm glad it was spared. There's an individuality about the place—melancholy it may be, perhaps dreary, as you say, but it isn't commonplace, so it misses the worst dreariness of all." He recurred to his first idea. "I wonder who will live there now poor old Hayes is dead."

"Rats," said Reynold. "And perhaps an old man and his wife, to take care of it."

Scarlett stood, with a shadow on his pleasant face. He had meant to go back to Mitchelhurst quite early in the summer, and he slipped a hand into his pocket, and fingered the little bundle of printed leaves which had played a part in his day-dream. He had counted on a welcome from the white-haired old gentleman, whose whims and oddities he understood and did not dislike, and he had waited contentedly enough till the time should come. In fact, he had found plenty to do that winter, what with Christmas visits, and the preparation of his poems for the press. As Adrian looked back, he realised that it had been a very agreeable winter, and that it had slipped away very quickly. The thought of Mitchelhurst had been there through it all, but, to tell the truth, it had not been very prominent. He would have spoken to Barbara in the autumn, if he had been left to himself, yet he had recognised the wisdom of the old man's prohibition, he had enjoyed the pathos of that unspoken farewell, and the sonnet which he touched and retouched with dainty grieving, and he had looked forward, very happily, to the end of his probation. Barbara, who was certainly very young, was growing a little older while he waltzed, and sang, and polished his rhymes, and made new friends wherever he went. Adrian had too much honesty to pretend to himself that he had been broken- hearted in consequence of their separation. He had not even felt uneasy, for, without being boastful, he had been very frankly and simply sure of the end of his love-story. He knew Barbara liked him.

And now it seemed that his testy little white-haired friend had gone out of the great old house into a smaller dwelling-place, and he had been reckoning on a dead man's welcome. A welcome—to what? To the cold clay of Mitchelhurst churchyard? The week before Christmas—Scarlett remembered that he had been very busy the week before Christmas, helping in some theatricals at a country house. He had been called, and called again at the end of the performance. And just then, at Mitchelhurst, the curtain had fallen for ever on the little part which Mr. Hayes had played, and Barbara had looked on its black mystery.

He bit his lip impatiently. There had been no harm in the theatricals, just the usual joking and intimacy among the actors behind the scenes, and the usual love-making and embraces on the stage. Adrian's conscience was clear enough, and yet the recollection of the girl who played the heroine (painted and powdered a little more than was absolutely necessary, for the mere pleasure of painting and powdering, as is the way with amateurs), came back to him with unpleasant distinctness. He could see her face, close to his own, as he remembered it on the hot little gaslit stage, in their great reconciliation scene, the scene that was always followed by a burst of applause. Everybody had admired his very becoming dress, and Scarlett himself had been rather proud of it. But now in a freak of his vivid imagination, he pictured the masquerading figure that he was, all showy pretence, with a head full of cues and inflated speeches, set down suddenly in the wintry loneliness of Mitchelhurst Place, and passing along the corridors to the threshold of the dead man's room, to see Barbara turn with startled eyes in the midst of the shadows. God! how pitiful and incongruous was that frippery, as he saw it in his fancy, brought thus into the presence of the last reality!

And Barbara, had she wondered at his silence during all these months? Never one word of regret for the old man who had been kind to him! "I wouldn't have had it happen for anything!" he said to himself. "What has she thought of me?"

Harding, with eyelids slightly drooping, was watching him, and Scarlett suddenly became aware of the fact.

"No, I suppose nobody is likely to take the old house," he said hurriedly. "I used to think it must be dull for Miss Strange, shut up there with nobody but her uncle."

"I should say it was."

"Well, Devonshire's a nice county, not that I know much of it. What part of Devonshire do the Stranges live in—do you know?"

"North Devon," Reynold Harding answered, and then added, half reluctantly, "Sandmoor, near Ilfracombe."

"Ah, it isn't a part I know at all," said Adrian aloud, and to himself he repeated "Sandmoor, near Ilfracombe."

At that moment the door opened, and one of the daughters of the house came in. "Oh, Mr. Harding!" she exclaimed, advancing, and shaking hands in a quick, careless fashion, "I'm afraid you've been kept waiting a long while."

"It doesn't matter," said Harding, standing very stiffly. "Is Guy ready now, Miss Wilton?"

"Yes, he's waiting in the hall. Bob got him away to the stables, and I didn't know he was there till just now: you know what those boys are when they get together. I thought Guy had *better* wait in the hall, for I'm afraid he's not as clean as he might be."

"It doesn't matter," Harding replied again. "He very seldom is."

"I did try to brush him," said the girl good-humouredly, "but I didn't do much good."

"Wanted something a good deal more thorough, no doubt," Adrian suggested.

"I hope he delivered his message?" Harding inquired. "It is his birthday to-morrow, and his father is going to take him for the day to the seaside. He was to ask if your brother would go with him."

"Oh, Bob will be delighted, I'm sure," said Miss Wilton. "I should think *you* would enjoy the holiday, Mr. Harding, you must be thankful to get rid of your charge now and then."

Scarlett, sitting on the end of the sofa, saw Harding's face darken with displeasure. "It makes very little difference, thank you," said the tutor coldly. "I think I'll go and find Guy now." And he bowed himself out of the room in his sullen fashion. The girl looked after him, and then turned to Adrian and laughed.

"Aren't we dignified?" she said. "What did I say to make him so cross? I didn't mean any harm."

"Oh, I don't know—I don't think you said anything very dreadful. Who is Guy?"

"Guy Robinson. His father has no end of money, Jones and Robinson the builders, you know, who are always getting big contracts for things in the newspapers—you see their names for ever. Old Robinson has bought the Priory, so they are neighbours of ours. Guy is twelve or thirteen, the only boy, and they won't send him to school."

"Mr. Harding is his tutor?"

Miss Wilton nodded.

"I shouldn't much fancy him for mine," said Scarlett reflectively. "I'm rather inclined to pity Master Guy."

"You needn't," the girl made answer, glancing shrewdly. "I think Mr. Harding is there under false pretences."

"False pretences?"

"Yes. I believe they think he is stern, and will keep Guy in order, and my private conviction is that he does nothing of the kind. Nobody *could* keep Guy in order, without perpetual battles, and Mr. Robinson always ends the battles, by dismissing the tutor. I never hear of any battles with Mr. Harding."

"I see. You think he spoils the boy."

"Spoils him? Well, I think that in his supreme contempt for Guy and all the Robinsons, he just takes care that he doesn't drown himself, or blow himself up with gunpowder, or break his neck, and I don't believe he troubles himself any further. I wonder what made the boy want to go to the seaside."

"How far is it?"

"Well, about thirty miles if they go to Salthaven. There's a railway—I should think old Robinson will have a special. Bob will have a great deal too much to eat and drink, and he'll be ill the day after. And if he and Guy can think of any senseless mischief, they are sure to be up to it, and the old man will swagger and pay for the damage. Boys will be boys," said Miss Wilton, with pompous intonation.

Adrian laughed. "Perhaps Mr. Harding will go too."

"Oh no! I know he won't."

"How do you know?"

"Mr. Robinson won't take him. My belief is that he's rather afraid of Mr. Harding. Oh! there he goes with Guy, out by the garden way."

Scarlett looked over her shoulder. "What a handsome fellow he is!"

"Handsome?" Miss Wilton turned her head, and looked doubtfully at her companion.

"Yes. Don't you think so?"

"N-no. It never occurred to me. Do you mean it really, or are you laughing?"

"Of course I mean it. Didn't you ever look at him?"

"Why yes, often."

"Well, then?"

"I suppose his features are good, when one comes to think about them," said the girl, with a dubious expression in her eyes. "Yes, I suppose they are."

"I wish mine were anything like as good," said Scarlett, with dispassionate candour.

"You wish yours——" Miss Wilton began, and ended with an amazed and incredulous laugh which was exceedingly flattering. It was so evidently genuine.

"I don't think you half believe me now," he said. "But I assure you, if you were to ask an artist he would tell you——"

"An artist? Oh, I dare say an artist might say so. But I don't believe a *woman* would say that Mr. Harding was good-looking."

"How if *she* were an artist?"

"Oh, then she wouldn't count."

"But why wouldn't a woman think so?"

She paused to consider. "I don't know," she said, "and yet I do mean it, somehow. He may be handsome, but he doesn't seem like it. I think a woman would want him to seem as well as to be."

"Do you mean that she wouldn't admire him unless he gave himself airs? That's not very complimentary to the woman, you know."

Miss Wilton shook her head. "I don't mean that. He might not think about himself at all—I should like him all the better." She stood for a minute with her eyes raised to Adrian's, yet was plainly looking back at the image of Reynold Harding which she had called up for the purpose of analysis. At last, "He isn't a bit unconscious!" she exclaimed. "He is the *most* self-conscious man I know. I believe he is *always* thinking about himself!"

"If he is," said Scarlett, "as far as I could judge I should say he didn't enjoy it much." "That's it!" she said. "He doesn't find himself attractive, and so—no more do we. *Isn't* that it?"

He smiled. "There's something in the idea as far as it goes. But it doesn't alter his features, you know."

"Of course not. But we don't look at them."

Adrian stood, pulling his moustache, and still smiling. He was not afraid, yet he found it rather pleasant to be told that this picturesque tutor, who had been shut up in Mitchelhurst Place with Barbara, was not the kind of man to take a woman's fancy. It was pleasant, but of course it did not mean much. Molly Wilton might be perfectly right, and yet it would not mean much. It is easy to lay down general rules about women, and very clever rules they often are. The mistake is, in applying these admirable theories to any one particular woman— she is certain to be an exception. Scarlett, while he listened to his companion, did not forget that there are always women enough to supply a formidable minority.

"I say," Miss Wilton exclaimed, with a real kindling of interest in her face, "I'll just go and take off my hat, and then we might try over that duet, you know."

To this he readily assented, but when she left the room he lingered by the window, and presently ejaculated "Poor devil!" It is hardly necessary to say that he was not thinking of Molly Wilton, who assuredly was neither angel nor devil, but a bright, wholesome, rather substantial young woman.

CHAPTER VII.
TWO GLANCES.

After all it was not Molly Wilton who first came into the room where Adrian waited for the duet, but her elder sister, Amy. Each sister had her recognised province, in which she reigned supreme. Amy was the beauty of the family, and had a taste for poetry; Molly was musical and lively. This arrangement worked perfectly, and Molly admired her sister's charms, and her poetical sympathies, without a trace of jealousy, feeling quite sure that justice would be done to her if there were any question of music or repartee.

Adrian was not looking at his proofs when Miss Wilton came in. He was sitting on the sofa, with his legs stretched out before him, gazing into space, and thinking of Sandmoor, near Ilfracombe. It was absolutely necessary that he should put himself into communication with that place, but how was it to be done? Should he write that day, or should he go the next?

"Oh, I have interrupted you!" Miss Wilton ejaculated, and stopped just inside the door.

"Interrupted me! Not a bit of it! I was only——"

"You were thinking of that sonnet—I know you were!"

"No, really," said Adrian, almost wishing he *had* been thinking of that sonnet. "No, I wasn't. In fact I think the sonnet is pretty well finished."

"Is it? You must read it to me, won't you?" and she came forward eagerly, took a chair, and dropped into a graceful attitude of attention. She had a real taste for poetry, and the poet was also to her liking. This was not the first time that she had listened, with shining eyes and quickened breath, and had brought the colour to the young man's cheek by saying with soft earnestness, "I like that— O, I like that!" Adrian found it very pleasant to read his poems to Miss Wilton.

"If you like," he said. "If you are sure it won't bore you."

"Of course I like," she answered.

"It's the first sonnet of all, you know," he explained, "a sort of dedication. I didn't like the one I had, so I shall make them put this in instead." He pulled his papers out of his pocket, and took a leaf of manuscript from among the printed pages. "You must tell me what you think of it," he said, and cleared his throat.

At that moment Molly opened the door. She saw the state of affairs at a glance, and slipped into her place, as quietly as if she had come into church late, and spied a convenient free seat.

Adrian read—

> "Have not all songs been sung, all loves been told?
>   What shall I say when nought is left unsaid?
>   The world is full of memories of the dead,
>   Echoes, and relics. Here's no virgin gold,
>   But all assayed, none left for me to mould
>   Into new coin, and at your feet to shed,
>   Each piece is mint-marked with some poet's head,
>   Tested and rung in tributes manifold.

> "O for a single word should be mine own—
>   And not the homage of long-studied art,
>   Common to all, for you who stand apart!
>   O weariness of measures tried and known!
>   Yet in their rhythm, you—if you alone—
>   Should hear the passionate pulses of my heart!"

As he finished he lifted his eyes and looked at Amy. Where else should a young man look, to emphasise the meaning of his love-poem, except into a woman's sympathising eyes? But the look, mere matter of course as it was, startled and silenced her. "You—if you alone!" The words, spoken with the soft fulness of Adrian's pleasant voice, rang in her ears. A young woman whose attractions were recognised by all the family might very well be pardoned for not at once perceiving that the emphasis was purely artistic.

But the silence which would have been full of meaning for the lover, frightened the poet.

"You don't like it!" he exclaimed, anxiously.

"Oh yes, I do—I like it very much."

"But there is something wrong," Adrian persisted. "I am sure you don't like it."

"Indeed—indeed I do," the girl declared fervently, and Molly chimed in with an enthusiastic—

"Oh, Mr. Scarlett, it's charming!"

"It's very kind of you to say so," he replied, pocketing his sonnet and going towards the piano, still with a slightly troubled expression. "Shall we try that duet now?"

Molly's thoughts were very easily diverted from poetry. She set up the music; but just as she was about to strike the first note, an idea occurred to her, and spinning half round on the stool—

"Amy," she said, "do *you* call that Mr. Harding so very good-looking?"

Amy was taken by surprise.

"I? oh no!" she answered.

"There!" Molly exclaimed, looking up at Scarlett.

"Why, what do you mean?" Miss Wilton asked. "Somehow I can't fancy he'll live. Whenever I look at that man's face I think of death."

"What a queer idea!" said the younger sister reflectively. "Well, he certainly doesn't look strong, and I should think that Robinson boy would be enough to worry anybody into an early grave."

Adrian, standing by the piano, raised his eyes to the old mirror, as if he half expected to see the pale face with its watchful eyes below the gleaming surface of the glass. But it reflected only a vague confusion of curtain and wall-paper, and the feathery foliage of a palm.

"I say," said Molly, "had you met him before this morning, or did you introduce yourselves?"

"We introduced ourselves. I found he knew a place where I stayed last summer. Don't you remember," he said, looking across at Amy, "the old house I told you about?"

"I remember. Where you wrote that bit,'*Waiting by the Sundial*'?"

Scarlett nodded.

"Yes. Well, I found he knew it well—in fact it turned out that he was a connection——"

"What, of your friends there?"

"No, not of my friends, of the old family who used to have the place."

"Oh, your friends aren't the old family then?" said Molly.

"No, they are not. I ought to say they *were* not—there were only two of them," he added in an explanatory fashion, "old Mr. Hayes, and his niece Miss Strange, and Mr. Harding told me to-day that the old man was dead. I didn't know it."

Molly looked up sympathetically, but, as he did not seem to be over-powered with grief, she went on, after a moment—

"Isn't it funny how, when one has never heard a name, and then one *does* hear it, one is sure to hear it again in three or four different ways directly? Did you ever notice that?"

Mr. Scarlett wasn't sure that he had, but he agreed that it was a very remarkable law.

"Well it always *is* so—you notice," she said. "Now I don't remember that I ever knew of anybody of the name of Strange in all my life, and now the Ashfords have got a Miss Strange staying with them, and here your friend is a Miss Strange."

His glance quickened a little at this illustration of the rule in question.

"Curious!" he said. "And who is this Miss Strange who is staying with the Ashfords?"

"Oh, she is a clergyman's daughter from Devonshire. She is very pretty. Amy, don't you think that Miss Strange is pretty?"

"Very pretty," said Amy, taking a book from the table.

"Yes, very pretty, for that style," Molly repeated.

"And what is her particular style?" Adrian asked, keeping his eyes, which were growing eager, fixed upon the keyboard.

"Oh, I don't know—she's rather small," said Molly lamely (Barbara was not as tall as Amy Wilton), "and she is dark—too dark, I think." (Amy was decidedly fair.) "She has a quantity of black hair. Do you like black hair?" (Amy's was wound in shining golden coils,) "and rather a colour, and fine eyes. Oh, dear, how *difficult* it is to describe people!"

It might be so, and yet young Scarlett, as he listened, could actually see a pair of soft eyes shining under darkly pencilled brows, a cloud of shadowy hair, and lips of deep carnation. It would rather have seemed that Miss Molly Wilton excelled in the art of description.

"Do you know what her name is?" he asked in an indifferent voice, stooping a little to look at a speck on one of the keys, and touching it with a neat fingernail.

"What, do you think it may be your Miss Strange?"

"It's possible," he said. "Her people were somewhere in that part of the world."

"I did hear her name—no, don't say it! Amy, do you remember Miss Strange's name?"

Amy looked up absently.

"Something old-fashioned—wasn't it Barbara?"

Adrian had lifted his head, and their eyes met. In that moment the girl saw what a glance could mean. It was just a flash of light, and then his ordinary look.

"Yes," he said, "that's the name; it must be the Miss Strange I know."

"Dear me!" said Molly, "I hope I didn't say any harm of her just now! You'd better go and call. You remember the Ashfords, you went with us to a garden party at their place when you were staying here two years ago."

Adrian smiled, and moved towards the window, forgetting his engagement at the piano.

"Oh!" said the disappointed musician, "aren't we to have the duet then?"

"I beg your pardon," he answered, coming back with bright promptitude, "I'm quite ready."

But Amy, as their voices rose and filled the room, sat gazing at the page which she did not read. She had seen how Adrian Scarlett could look, when he heard the name of Barbara. And she had thought, because he turned towards her when he read a sonnet—she had thought—what? A pink flush dyed her delicate skin. Our pardonable mistakes are precisely what we ourselves can never pardon.

The song being ended young Scarlett made his escape. He was half amused, half indignant.

"Sandmoor near Ilfracombe! Confound the fellow, he knew where she was all the time, and I thought he was rather unwilling to give me her Devonshire address! Sandmoor near Ilfracombe indeed!"

CHAPTER VIII

IN NUTFIELD LANE.

When Reynold Harding assured Miss Wilton that it made very little difference to him whether he got rid of his pupil for a day or not, he told a lie. From the moment when he heard of Guy's holiday, he had resolved in his own mind that on that day of freedom, he would see Barbara Strange.

He knew that she was staying with the Ashfords, and he had heard the Robinson girls talking about her one day after luncheon.

"That pretty little Devonshire girl finds it dull, I think," said Violet.

"Who wouldn't?" her sister exclaimed. "She has had time to hear all old Ashford's stories a dozen times before this, and they are stupid enough the first time. But how do you know she finds it dull?"

"They say she is always running about the fields looking for primroses and cowslips. I saw her when I was out riding this morning, leaning on the gate into Nutfield Lane, with her hands full of them."

"How very picturesque! Looking into the lane for some more?"

"Or for some one to help her carry what she'd got. I don't know what I mightn't be driven to, myself, if I had to listen to old Ashford's prosing, and then go crawling out for a couple of hours boxed up in Mother Ashford's stuffy old brougham, two or three times a week. And Willy Ashford hardly ever comes, now he's engaged to that girl in Kensington."

"No," said Muriel, "and I don't know that he would mend matters much if he did. Well, perhaps somebody with a taste for cowslips and innocence, will happen to walk along Nutfield Lane next time Miss Strange is looking over the gate. What did you think of doing this afternoon?"

They were standing in the window, and speaking low. But their voices were metallic and penetrating, and the tutor, who was watching Guy's progress through a meal, which had worn out his sisters' patience, heard every word. He had his back to the light, and the boy did not see the black full veins on his forehead.

"But I want some more tart," said Guy.

The request was granted with careless liberality.

"Is that enough?" Harding asked.

The boy eyed it. He did not think he could possibly manage any more, but he said—

"I don't know," just as a measure of precaution.

"Well, eat that first," said the other, and sat, resting his head on his hand.

He knew Nutfield Lane. It was three or four miles from the Priory; Guy and he went that way sometimes. He remembered a gate there, with posts set close to a couple of towering elms, that arched it with their budding boughs, and thrust their roots above the trodden pathway. There was a meadow beyond, the prettiest possible background for a pretty little Devonshire girl with her hands full of cowslips. As to her looking out for any one—he would like to walk straight up to those vulgar, chattering, expensive young women, and knock their heads together. It seemed to Harding that there would be something very soothing and satisfying about such an expression of his opinion, if only it were possible! But it could not be, and he relinquished the thought with a sigh, as he had relinquished the pursuit of other unattainable joys.

"N—no, I don't want any more," said Guy, regretfully. "Only some more beer."

Harding nodded, with that absent-minded acquiescence which had endeared him to his pupil. Guy was only to him like a buzzing fly, or any other tiresome little presence, to be endured in silence, and, as far as possible, ignored. But when that afternoon the boy came to him with the announcement that he should be twelve on Tuesday, and his father was going to take him somewhere for the whole day, Reynold raised his head from the exercise he was correcting, and looked at him fixedly.

"That's all right," he said, after a moment.

In that moment he had made up his mind. He wanted to see Barbara. And then? He did not know what then, but he wanted to see her.

The white spring sunshine lighted the page which Guy had scrawled and blotted, and Reynold sat with the pen between his fingers, dreaming. He would see Barbara, but he would not even attempt to think what he would do or say when they met. He had planned and schemed before, and chance had swept all his schemes away. Now he would leave it all to chance; it was enough for him to think that he would certainly see her again.

He would see her, not standing as he had seen her first, in sad autumnal scenery, not coming towards him in the pale firelit room, not walking beside him to the village, while the wind drove flights of dead leaves across the grey curtain of the sky, not as she faced him, frightened and breathless, in the quivering circle of lamplight on the stairs, not as he remembered her last of all, when she stood beyond the boundary which he might not cross, and Mitchelhurst Place rose behind her in the light of the moon, white and dead as dry bones. It seemed to him that it must always be autumn at Mitchelhurst, with dim, short days, and gusty nights, and the chilly atmosphere laden with odours of decay. But all this was past and over, and he was going to meet Barbara in the spring. Barbara in April—all happy songs of love, all the young gladness of the year, all tender possibilities were summed up in those three words. He was startled at the sudden eagerness which escaped from his control, and throbbed and bounded within him when he resolved to see her once again. But he did not betray it outwardly, unless, perhaps, by an attempt to write his next correction with a dry pen.

He listened to Guy's excited chatter as the day drew near, and set out with him to carry the invitation to Bob Wilton, in a mood which, on the surface, was one of apathetic patience. Nothing he could do would hasten the arrival of Tuesday, but nevertheless it was coming. When the two boys went off to the stables together, he waited. He might as well wait in the Wiltons' sunny drawing-room as anywhere else. And when some one entered by the further door and began to play, he listened, not ill pleased. He had no ear for music, but the defect was purely physical, and except for that hindrance he might have loved it. As it was he could not appreciate the meaning of what was played beyond the curtain, nor could he recognise the skill and delicacy with which it was rendered. To him it was only a bright, formless ripple of sound, gliding vaguely by, till suddenly Barbara's tune, rounded and clear and silver sweet, awoke him from his reverie.

For a moment he sat breathless with wonder. Only a dull memory of her music had stayed with him, a kind of tuneless beating of its measure, and the living notes, melodiously full, pursued that poor ghost through his heart and brain. His pulses throbbed as if the girl herself were close at hand. Then he rose, and softly stepped across the room. Who was it who was playing Barbara's tune? Who but the man who had played it to Barbara?

Considered as a piece of reasoning this was weak. Anybody would have told him the name of the composer, and could have assured him that dozens and scores of men might play the thing. Barbara might have heard it on a barrel organ! But Harding's thoughts went straight to the one man who had left music lying about at Mitchelhurst with his name, "Adrian Scarlett," written on it. Barbara's tune jangled wildly in his ears; she had learnt it from this man, or she had taught it to him.

Thus it happened that Adrian looked up from his playing, and saw the picture in the mirror, the face that followed him with its intent and hostile gaze. And

Reynold, standing apart and motionless, watched the musician, and noted his air of careless ease and mastery, the smile which lingered on his lips, and the way in which he threw back his head and let his glances rove, though of course he did not know that all these things were a little accentuated by Adrian's self-consciousness under his scrutiny. He was sure, even before a word had been uttered, that this was the man whose name had haunted him at Mitchelhurst, and who won Mr. Pryor's heart by singing at his penny reading. To Reynold, standing in the shadow, Scarlett was the type of the conquering young hero, swaggering a little in the consciousness of his popularity and his facile triumphs.

To some extent he wronged Adrian, and on one point Adrian wronged him. He believed that Harding had exulted in the idea of putting him on the wrong scent with his "Sandmoor near Ilfracombe." But in point of fact Harding had given the address with real reluctance. He had been asked where the Stranges lived, and had told the truth. To have supplemented it with information as to Barbara's whereabouts would have been to assume a knowledge of Scarlett's meaning in asking the question, a thing intolerable and impossible. Yet Harding's morbid pride was galled by his unwilling deceit, and he wished that the subject had never been mentioned. He had no doubt that his rival would go to Sandmoor, but he did not exult in the thought of the disappointment that awaited him there.

Still, when Tuesday came it undoubtedly was a satisfaction to feel that the express was carrying Mr. Scarlett further and further from the gate which led into Nutfield Lane. Otherwise the day was of but doubtful promise, its blue blotted with rain-clouds, which Guy Robinson regarded as a personal injury. It brightened, however, after the birthday party had started, and Reynold set out on his rather vague errand, under skies which shone and threatened in the most orthodox April fashion. The heavens might have laid a wager that they would show a dozen different faces in the hour, from watery sadness to glittering joy. It was hardly a day on which Mrs. Ashford would care to creep out in her brougham, but a little Devonshire girl, tired of a dull house, might very well face it with an umbrella and her second-best hat.

Harding made sure that she would. If she failed to do so he had no scheme ready. He did not know the Ashfords, and to go up to their house and ask for Miss Strange, could lead, at the best, to nothing but a formal interview under the eyes of an old lady who would consider his visit an impertinence. But Barbara would come! It was surely time that his luck should turn. When the hazard of the die has been against us a dozen times we are apt to have an irrational conviction that our chance must come with the next throw, and Harding strolled round the Ashfords' place, questioning only how, and how soon, she would appear. To see her once—it was so little that he asked!—to see her, and to hold her hand for a moment in his own, and to make her look up at him, straight into his eyes. And if she had the fancy still, as he somehow thought she had, to hear him say that he forgave her, why, he would say it. As if he had ever blamed her for the little forgetfulness which had ended all his hopes of fortune! And yet, if Barbara could have known how near that fortune had been! The old man's health had failed suddenly during the winter, the great inheritance was about to fall in, and Reynold would have been a partner and his own master within a few months from his decision. "Well," he said to himself as he leant on the gate in Nutfield Lane, "and even so, what harm has she done? Was I not going to say No before I saw her? And if she persuaded me to write the Yes which turned to No at the bottom of her apron pocket, am I to complain of her for that?"

He thought, that he would ask her for a flower, a leaf, or a budding twig from the hedge, just by way of remembrance. At present he had none, except the unopened letter which she had given back to him in his lodgings at Mitchelhurst.

The day grew fairer as it passed. Though a couple of sparkling showers, which filled the sunlit air with the quick flashing of falling drops, drove him once and again for shelter to a hay-stack in a neighbouring meadow, the blue field overhead widened little by little, and shone through the tracery of leafless boughs. He felt his spirits rising almost in spite of himself. He came back, after the second shower, by the field path to the lane, and was in the act of getting over the gate when he heard steps coming quickly towards him. Not Barbara's, they were from the opposite direction. He sprang hastily down, and found himself face to face with Mr. Adrian Scarlett, who was humming a tune.

Reynold drew a long breath, and stood as if he were turned to stone. Adrian was only mortal, he lifted his hat, and smiled his greeting, with a look in his grey-blue eyes which said as plainly as possible, "*Didn't you think I was at Sandmoor?*" and then walked on towards the Ashfords' house, where he had been to the tennis party two years before. He would be very welcome there. And if he should chance to meet Barbara by the way, *he* knew very well what he was going to say to her. But a moment later he felt a touch of pity for the luckless fellow who had not outwitted him after all. "Poor devil!" he said, as he had said the day before.

The epithet, which, like many another, is flung about inappropriately enough, hit the mark for once. Reynold stood pale and dumb, choked with bitter hate, but helpless and hopeless enough for pity. He would do no more with hate than he had done with love. He knew it, and presently he turned and walked drearily away. He did not want to see Barbara when she had met Adrian Scarlett. He had meant to see her *first*, to end his unlucky little love-story with a few gentle words, to hold her hand for a moment, and then to step aside and leave her free to go her way. What harm would there have been? But this man, who was to have everything, had baulked him even in this. She would not care for his pardon now, and perhaps it would hardly have been worth taking. If one is compelled to own one's forgiveness superfluous it is difficult to keep it sweet.

So he did not see Barbara when, a little later, she came up Nutfield Lane by Scarlett's side. They stopped by the gate, and leant on it. Barbara had no flowers in her hands, but it seemed to her that all the country-side was blossoming.

She looked a little older than when Adrian had bidden her his mute farewell at Mitchelhurst. The expression of her face was at once quickened and deepened, her horizon was enlarged, though the gaze which questioned it was as innocent as ever. But her dark eyes kept a memory of the proud patience with which she had waited through the winter. There had been times when her faith in the *Clergy List* had been shaken, and she had doubted whether Adrian would ever consult its pages, and find out where her father lived. She did not blame him; he was free as air; yet those had been moments of almost unbearable loneliness. She never spoke of him to anybody; to have been joked and pitied by Louisa and Hetty would have been hateful to her. She thought of him continually, and dreamed of him sometimes. But there was only a limited satisfaction in dreaming of Adrian Scarlett; he was apt to be placed in absurdly topsy-turvy circumstances, and to behave unaccountably. Barbara felt, regretfully, that a girl who was parted from such a lover should have dreamed in a loftier manner. She was ashamed of herself, although she knew she could not help it. Now, however, there was no need to trouble herself about dreams or clergy lists; Adrian was leaning on the gate by her side.

"What you must have thought of me!" he was saying. "Never to take the least notice of your uncle's death! I can't think how I missed hearing of it."

"It was in the *Times* and some of the other papers," said Barbara.

The melancholy little announcement had seemed to her a sort of appeal to her absent lover.

"I never saw it. I was—busy just then," he explained with a little hesitation. "I suppose I didn't look at the papers. I have been fancying you at Mitchelhurst all the time, and promising myself that I would go back there, and find you where I found you first."

Barbara did not speak; she leaned back and looked up at him with a smile.

Adrian's answering gaze held hers as if it enfolded it.

"I *might* have written," he said, "or inquired—I might have done *something*, at any rate! I can't think how it was I didn't! But I'd got it into my head that I wanted to get those poems of mine out—wanted to go back to you with my volume in my hand, and show you the dedication. I was waiting for that—I never thought——"

"Yes," said the girl with breathless admiration and approval. "And are they finished now?"

"Confound the poems!" cried Adrian with an amazed, remorseful laugh. A stronger word had been on his lips. "Don't talk of them, Barbara! To think that I neglected you while I was polishing those idiotic rhymes, and that you think it was all right and proper! Oh, my dear, if you tried for a week you couldn't make me feel smaller! If—if anything had happened to you, and I had been left with my trumpery verses—"

"You shall not call them that! Don't talk so!"

"Well, suppose you had got tired of waiting, and had come across some better fellow. There was time enough, and it would have served me right."

"I don't know about serving you right, but there wouldn't have been time for me to get tired of waiting," said Barbara, and added more softly, "not if it had been all my life."

"Listen to that!" Adrian answered, leaning backward, with his elbows on the gate. "All her life—for *me*!"

His quick fancy sketched that life: first the passionate eagerness, throbbing, hoping, trusting, despairing; then submission to the inevitable, the gradual extinction of expectation as time went on; and finally the dimness and placidity of old age, satisfied to worship a pathetic memory. Hardly love, rather love's ghost, that shadowy sentiment, cut off from the strong actual existence of men and women, and thinly nourished on recollections, and fragments of mild verse. Scarlett turned away, as from a book of dried flowers, to Barbara.

"What did you think of me?" he said, still dwelling on the same thought. "Never one word!"

"Well, I felt as if there were a word—at least, a kind of a word—once," she said. "I went with Louisa to the dentist last February—it was Valentine's Day —she wanted a tooth taken out. There were some books and papers lying about in the waiting-room. One of them was an old Christmas number, with something of yours in it. Do you remember?"

"N—no," said Scarlett doubtfully.

"Oh, don't say it wasn't yours! A little poem—it had your name at the end. There can't be *another*, surely," said Barbara, with a touch of resentment at the idea. "There were two illustrations, but I didn't care much for them; I didn't think they were good enough. I read the poem over and over. I did so hope I should recollect it all; but he was ready for Louisa before I had time to learn it properly, and our name was called. It was a very bad tooth, and Louisa had gas, you know. I was obliged to go. I am so slow at learning by heart. Louisa would have known it all in half the time; but I did wish I could have had just one minute more."

"Tell me what it was," Adrian said.

"*My love loves me*," Barbara began in a timid voice.

"Oh—that! Yes, I remember now. The man who edits that magazine is a friend of mine, and he asked me for some little thing for his Christmas number. If I had thought you would have cared I could have sent it to you."

Her eyes shone with grateful happiness.

"But I didn't," said Adrian. "I didn't do anything. Well, go on, Barbara, tell me how much you remembered."

Barbara paused a moment, looking back to the open page on the dentist's green table-cloth. As she spoke she could see poor Louisa, awaiting her summons with a resigned and swollen face, an old gentleman examining a picture in the *Illustrated London News* through his eyeglass, and a lady apprehensively turning the pages of the dentist's pamphlet, *On Diseases of the Teeth and Gums*. Outside, the rain was streaming down the window panes. Barbara recalled all this with Adrian's verses.

> "*My love loves me. Then wherefore care*
> *For rain or shine, for foul or fair?*
> *My love loves me.*
> *My daylight hours are golden wine,*
> *And all the happy stars are mine,*
> *My love loves me!*"

"*Love flies away*," she began more doubtfully, and looked at Adrian, who took it up.

> *"Love flies away, and summer mirth*
> *Lies cold and grey upon the earth,*
> *Love flies away,*
> *The sun has set, no more to rise,*
> *And far, beneath the shrouded sides,*
> *Love flies away."*

"Yes!" cried Barbara, "that's it! I had forgotten those last lines—how stupid of me!"

"Not at all," said Adrian. "You remembered all that concerned you, the rest was quite superfluous."

"Oh, but how I did try to remember the end!" she continued pensively. "It haunted me. If I had only had a minute more! But all the same I felt as if I had had something of a message from you that day. It was my valentine, wasn't it?"

Scarlett's eyes, with a look half whimsical, half touched with tender melancholy, met hers.

"I *wish* we were worth a little more—my poems and I!" said he. "I wish I were a hero, and had written an epic. Yes, by Jove! an epic in twelve books."

"Oh, not for me!" cried Barbara.

CHAPTER IX.
A VERSE OF AN OLD SONG.

"Adrian!"

The name was uttered with just a hint of hesitating appeal.

"At your service," Scarlett answered promptly. He had a bit of paper before him, and was pencilling an initial letter to be embroidered on Barbara's handkerchiefs.

"Adrian, did you hear that Mr. Harding—you know whom I mean—was ill?"

"Yes, I did hear something about it." He put his head on one side and looked critically at his work. "Is it anything serious?"

"Yes," said Barbara. "I'm afraid it is."

"Poor fellow! I'm very sorry. How the days do shorten, don't they?"

"Yes," said Barbara again. "They spoke as if he were going to—die."

"Really? I'm sorry for that. It is strange," Adrian continued, putting in a stroke very delicately, "but one of the Wilton girls used always to say he looked like it. I think it was Molly."

Barbara sighed but did not speak.

"Let's see," said Adrian, "he left the Robinsons—what happened? Didn't the boy get drowned?"

"No!" scornfully, "he fell into the water, but somebody fished him out."

"Not Harding?"

"No, somebody else. Mr. Harding went in, but he couldn't swim, and he didn't reach Guy. But he got a chill—it seems that was the beginning of it all."

Scarlett leant back in his chair, twirling the pencil between his fingers and looking at Barbara, whose eyes were fixed upon the rug. They were alone in the drawing-room of a house in Kensington. Their wedding was to be in about six weeks' time, and Barbara was staying for a fortnight with an aunt who had undertaken to help her in her shopping—a delightful aunt who paid bills, and who liked a quiet nap in the afternoon. Adrian sometimes went out with them, and always showed great respect for the good lady's slumbers.

"Well," he said, after a pause, "and where is Mr. Harding now?"

"At his mother's. She lives at Westbourne Park."

"Westbourne Park," Scarlett repeated. "By Jove, that's a change from Mitchelhurst! A nice healthy neighbourhood, and convenient for Whiteley's, I suppose; but *what* a change! I say, Barbara, how do you happen to know so much about the Hardings?"

"Adrian!"

And again she seemed to appeal and hesitate in the mere utterance of his name. She crossed the room, and touched his shoulder with her left hand, which had a ring shining on it—a single emerald, a point of lucid colour on her slim finger.

"Adrian, I wanted to ask you, would there be any harm if——"

"No," said Adrian gravely, "no harm at all. Not the slightest. Certainly not."

He took her other hand in his.

She looked doubtfully at him.

"What do you mean?"

"What do *you* mean, Barbara?"

"I wanted to go to the door and ask how he is—that's all. I feel as if I shouldn't like to go away without a word. We didn't part quite good friends, you know. And last year he was making his plans, and now we are making ours, and he——Oh, Adrian, why is life so sad? And yet I never thought I *could* be as happy as I am now."

"It's rather mixed, isn't it?" he said, smiling up at her, and he drew her hand to his lips. Barbara's eyes were full of tears. To hide them, she stooped quickly and touched his hair with a fleeting kiss.

"By all means go and ask after your friend before you leave town," said Adrian. "Let us hope he isn't as bad as they think."

"He is," said the girl. Long before this she had told Adrian about her night adventure at Mitchelhurst. She had been perfectly frank about it, and yet she sometimes doubted her own confession. It seemed so little when she spoke of it to him, so unimportant, so empty of all meaning. Could it be that, and only that, which had troubled her so strangely? He had smiled as he listened, and had put it aside. "I don't suppose you did very much harm," he said, "but any one with half an eye could see that he wasn't the kind of fellow to take things easily. Poor Barbara!" She stood now with something of the same perplexity on her brow; the thought of Reynold Harding always perplexed her.

There was a brief silence, during which she abandoned her hands to Adrian's clasp, and felt his touch run through her, from sensitive finger tips to her very heart. Then she spoke quickly, yet half unwillingly, "Very well then, I shall go."

"You wish it?" Adrian exclaimed, swift to detect every shade of meaning in her voice. "Because, if not, there is no reason why you should. If you hadn't said just now you wanted to go——"

She drew one hand away and turned a little aside. "I know," she said, "I did say it. Really and truly I don't want to go; it makes me uncomfortable to think about him, but I want to have been."

"Get it over then. Ask, and come away as quickly as you can."

"To-morrow?" said Barbara. "I thought, perhaps, as aunt was not going with us about those photograph frames, that to-morrow might do. I couldn't go with aunt."

"You have thought of everything. Go on."

"You might put me into a cab after we leave the shop," she continued. "I think that would be best. I would go and just inquire, and then come straight on here. I don't want to explain to anybody, and if you say it is all right——"

"Why, it is all right, of course. That's settled then," said Adrian.

The next day was dreary even for late November. Adrian and Barbara passed through the frame-maker's door into an outer gloom, chilly and acrid with a touch of fog, and variegated with slowly-descending blacks. Everything was dirty and damp. There were gas-lights in the shop windows of a dim tawny yellow.

Scarlett looked right and left at the sodden street and then upward in the direction of the sky. "This isn't very nice," he said; "hadn't we better go straight home?"

"No—please!" Barbara entreated. "We have filled up to-morrow and the next day, and aunt has asked some people to afternoon tea on Saturday."

"All right; it may be better when we get to Westbourne Park. I'll go a bit of the way with you."

He looked for a cab. Barbara waited passively by his side, gazing straight before her. She had never looked prettier than she did at that moment, standing on the muddy step in the midst of the universal dinginess. Excitement had given tension and brilliancy to her face, she was flushed and warm in her wrappings of dark fur, and above the rose-red of her cheeks her eyes were shining like stars. "Here we are!" said Scarlett, as he hailed a loitering hansom.

They drove northward, passing rows of shops, all blurred and glistening in the foggy air, and wide, muddy crossings, where people started back at the driver's hoarse shout. Scarlett, with Barbara's hand in his, watched the long procession of figures on the pavement—dusky figures which looked like marionnettes, going mechanically and ceaselessly on their way. To the young man, driving by at his ease, their measured movements had an air of ineffectual toil; they were on the treadmill, they hurried for ever, and were always left behind. Looking at them he thought of the myriads in the rear, stepping onward, stepping continually. If they had really been marionnettes! But the droll thing was that each figure had a history; there was a world- picture in every one of those little, jogging heads.

Presently the shops became scarce, the procession on the pavement grew scattered and thin. They were driving up long, dim streets of stuccoed houses. They passed a square or two where trees, black and bare, rose above shadowy masses of evergreens all pent together within iron railings. One might have fancied that the poor things had strayed into the smoky wilderness, and been impounded in that melancholy place.

"We must be almost there," said Adrian at last, when they had turned into a cross street where the plastered fronts were lower and shabbier. He put the question to the cabman.

"Next turning but one, sir," was the answer.

"Then I'll get out here," said Scarlett.

Barbara murmured a word of farewell, but she felt that it was best. She always thought of Reynold Harding as the unhappiest man she knew, and she could not have driven up to his door to flaunt her great happiness before his eyes. She leant forward quickly, and caught a glimpse of that clear happiness of hers on the side walk, smiling and waving a farewell, the one bright and pleasant thing to look upon in the grey foulness of the afternoon.

A turning—then it was very near indeed! Another dull row of houses, each with its portico and little flight of steps. Here and there was a glimmer of gas-light in the basement windows. Then another corner and they were in the very street, and going more slowly as the driver tried to make out the numbers on the doors. At that moment it suddenly occurred to Miss Strange that her errand was altogether absurd and impossible. She was seized with an overpowering paroxysm of shyness. Her heart stood still, and then began to throb with labouring strokes. Why had she ever come?

Had it depended on herself alone she would certainly have turned round and gone home, but the cab stopped with a jerk opposite one of the stuccoed houses, and there was an evident expectation that she would get out and knock at the door. What would the cabman think of her if she refused, and what could she say to Adrian after all the fuss she had made? Well, perhaps she could face Adrian, who always understood. But the cabman! She alighted and went miserably up the steps.

A servant answered her knock, and stood waiting. Between the maid and the man Barbara plucked up a desperate courage, and asked if Mrs. Harding was at home. She was.

"How is Mr. Harding to-day?" inquired Barbara, hesitating on the threshold.

"Much as usual, thank you, miss," the girl replied. "Won't you step in?"

She obeyed. After all, as she reflected, she need only stay a few minutes, and to go away with merely the formal inquiry, made and answered at the door, would be unsatisfactory. Mr. Harding might never hear that she had called. She followed the maid into a vacant sitting-room, and gave her a card to take to her mistress. The colour rushed to her very forehead as she opened the case. Her Uncle Hayes had had her cards printed with *Mitchelhurst Place* in the corner, and though, on coming to Kensington, she had drawn her pen through it, and written her aunt's address instead, it was plain enough to see. How would a Rothwell like to read *Mitchelhurst Place* on a stranger's card? She felt that she was a miserable little upstart.

Mrs. Harding did not come immediately, and Barbara as she waited was reminded of the dentist's room at Ilfracombe. "It's just like it," she said to herself, "and I can't have gas, so it's worse, really. And she hasn't got as many books either." This brought back a memory, and her lips and eyes began to smile—

> *"My love loves me. Then wherefore care*
> *For rain or shine, for foul or fair?*
> *My love loves me."*

But the smile was soon followed by a sigh.

The door opened and Mrs. Harding came in. To Barbara, still in her teens, Reynold's mother was necessarily an old woman, but she recognised her beauty almost in spite of herself, and stood amazed. Mrs. Harding wore black, and it was rather shabby black, but she had the air of a great lady, and her visitor, in her presence, was a shy blushing child. She apologised for her delay, and the apology was a condescension.

"You don't know me," said the girl in timid haste, "but I know Mr. Harding a little, and I thought I would call."

"Oh, yes," said Kate, "I know you by name, Miss Strange. My son was indebted to Mr. Hayes for an invitation to Mitchelhurst Place last autumn."

"I'm sure we were very glad," Barbara began, and then stopped confusedly, remembering that they had turned Mr. Reynold Harding out of the house before his visit was over. The situation was embarrassing. "I wish we could have made it pleasanter for him," she said, and blushed more furiously than ever.

"Have made Mitchelhurst Place pleasanter?" Mrs. Harding repeated. "Thank you, you are very kind. I believe he had a great wish to see the Place."

"It's a fine old house," said Barbara, conversationally. "I have left it now."

"So I supposed. I was sorry to see in the paper that Mr. Hayes was dead. I remember him very well, five-and-twenty or thirty years ago."

"I am going abroad," the girl continued. "I—I don't exactly know how long we shall be away. I am going to be married. But they told me Mr. Harding was ill—I hope it is not serious? I thought, as I was near, that I should like to ask before I went."

Mrs. Harding considered her with suddenly awakened attention. "He is very ill," she said, briefly. "You know what is the matter with him?"

"Yes, I suppose so."

"He was not very strong as a boy. At one time he seemed better, but it was only for a time."

"I'm very sorry," said Barbara, standing up. "Please tell him I came to ask how he was before I went."

Mrs. Harding rose too, and looked straight into her visitor's eyes. "Would you like to see him?"

"I don't know," the girl faltered. "I'm not sure he would care to see me. If he would—"

Mrs. Harding interrupted her, "Excuse me a moment," and vanished.

Barbara, left alone, stood confounded. She was taken by surprise, and yet she was conscious that to see Reynold Harding was what she had really been hoping and dreading from the first. Some one moved overhead. Perhaps he would say "No," in that harsh, sudden voice of his. Well, then, she would escape from this house, which was like a prison to her, and go back to Adrian, knowing that she had done all she could. Perhaps he would laugh, and say

"Yes."

She listened with strained attention. A chair was moved, a fire was stirred, a door was closed. Then her hostess reappeared. "Will you come this way?" she said.

Barbara obeyed without a word. The matter was taken out of her hands, and nothing but submission was possible. The grey dusk was gathering on the stairs, and through a tall window, rimmed with squares of red and blue, rose a view of roofs and chimneys half drowned in fog. Barbara passed onward and upward, went mutely through a door which was opened for her, and saw Reynold Harding sitting by the fire. He lifted his face and looked at her. In an instant there flashed into her memory a verse of the old song of *Barbara Allen*, sung to her as a child for her name's sake:—

> "*Slowly, slowly, she came up,*
>
> *And slowly she came nigh him;*
>
> *And all she said when there she came,*
>
> *'Young man, I think you're dying.'*"

The words, which she had sung to herself many a time, taking pleasure in their grotesque simplicity, presented themselves now with such sudden and ghastly directness, that a cold damp broke out on her forehead. She set her teeth fast, fearing that Barbara's speech would force its way through her lips with an outburst of hysterical laughter. What *could* she say, what could anybody say, but, "Young man, I think you're dying?" The words were clamouring so loudly in her ears that she glanced apprehensively at Mrs. Harding to make sure that they had not been spoken.

Reynold's smile recalled her to herself, and told her that he was reading too much on her startled face. "Won't you sit down?" he said, pointing to a chair. Before she took it she instinctively put out her hand, and greeted him with a murmur of speech. What she said she did not exactly know, but *not* those hideous words, thank God!

Mrs. Harding paused for a moment by the fire, gazing curiously at her son, as if she were studying a problem. Then silently, in obedience to some sign of his, or to some divination of her own, she turned away and left the two together.

Barbara looked over her shoulder at the closing door, and her eyes in travelling back to Harding's face took in the general aspect of the room. It was fairly large and lofty. Folding doors, painted a dull drab, divided it from what she conjectured was the sick man's bed-room. It was dull, it was negative, not particularly shabby, not uncomfortable, not vulgar, but hopelessly dreary and commonplace. There was in it no single touch of beauty or individuality on which the eye could rest. Some years earlier an upholsterer had supplied the ordinary furniture, a paper-hanger had put up an ordinary paper, and, except that time had a little dulled and faded everything, it remained as they had left it. The drab was rather more drab, that was all.

"Well," said Reynold from his arm-chair, "so you have come to see me."

"I wanted to ask you how you were—I heard you were ill," Barbara explained, and it struck her that she was exactly like a little parrot, saying the same thing over and over again.

"Very kind of you," he replied. "Do you want me to answer?"

"If—if you could say you were getting a little better."

He smiled. "It looks like it, doesn't it?" he said, languidly.

Barbara's eyes met his for a moment, and then she hung her head.

No, it did not look like it. Two candles were burning on the chimney-piece, but the curtains had not been drawn. Between the two dim lights, yellow and grey, he sat, leaning a little sideways, with a face like the face of the dead, except for the great sombre eyes which looked out of it, and the smile which showed a glimpse of his teeth. His hand hung over the arm of his chair, the hot nerveless hand which Barbara had taken in her own a moment before.

"I am so sorry," she said. "I hoped I might have had some better news of you before I went away. Did you know I was going away—going to be married?"

She looked up, putting the question in a timid voice, and he answered "Yes," with a slight movement of his head and eyelids. "I wish you all happiness."

"Thank you," said Barbara gratefully.

"And where are you going?"

"To Paris for a time, and then we shall see. He"—this with a little hesitation —"he is very busy."

"Busy—what, more poems?" said the man who had done with being busy.

"Yes. Did you see his volume?"

Harding shook his head. "I'm afraid I'm a little past Mr. Scarlett's poetry."

"Oh!" said Barbara, "of course one can't read when one is ill. You ought to rest."

"Yes," he assented, "I don't seem able to manage that either, just at present, but I dare say I shall soon. Meanwhile I sit here and look at the fire."

"Yes," said the girl. "Some people see all sorts of things in the fire."

"So they say," he answered listlessly. "*I* see it eating its heart out slowly. And so you are going to Paris? That was your dream when you were at Mitchelhurst."

"Yes—you told me to wait, and it would come, and it is coming. Oh, but you had dreams at Mitchelhurst, too, Mr. Harding! I wanted them to come true as well as mine."

"Did you? That was very kind of you. Mitchelhurst was a great place for dreams, wasn't it? But I left mine there. Better there."

"I felt ashamed just now," said Barbara, "when your mother spoke about your staying with us at Mitchelhurst. She doesn't know, then? Oh, Mr. Harding, I hate to think how we treated you in your old home, and I know my poor uncle was sorry too!"

"What for? People who can't agree are better apart, and Mrs. Simmonds' lodgings were comfortable enough," said Reynold.

"Oh, but it wasn't right! If you and uncle had only met—"

"Well, if all they tell us is true, I suppose we shall before long. Let's hope we may both be better tempered."

"Don't!" cried Barbara, with a glance at the pale face opposite, and a remembrance of her Uncle Hayes propped up in the great bed at Mitchelhurst. Would those two spectres meet and bow, in some dim underworld of graves and skeletons? She could not picture them glorified in any way, could not fancy them otherwise than as she had known them. "Pray don't," she said again.

"Very well," said Reynold, "but why not? It makes no difference. Still, talk of what you please."

"Does it hurt you to talk?"

"Yes, I believe it does. Everything hurts me, and therefore nothing does. So if you like it any better, it doesn't."

"I won't keep you long," said Barbara. "Perhaps I ought not to have come, but I felt as if I could not leave England without a word. You see, there is no knowing how long I may be away—"

"You were wise," said Reynold. "A pleasant journey to you! But don't come here to look for me when you come back. The fire will be out, and the room will be swept and garnished. This is a very chilly room when it is swept and garnished."

To Barbara it was a dim and suffocating room at that moment. She hardly felt as if it were really she who sat there, face to face with that pale Rothwell shadow, and she put up her hand and loosened the fur at her throat.

"You do not mind my coming now?" she said, ignoring the latter half of his speech. "You remember that evening? You did not make me very welcome then." A tremulous little laugh ended the sentence.

He shifted his position in the big chair with a weary effort, and let his head fall back. "It's different," he said. "Everything is different. I was alive then— five-and-twenty—and I was afraid you might get yourself into some trouble on my account—you had told me how the Mitchelhurst people gossipped. *I* understood, but they wouldn't have. Did the old man hear of it?"

"No," said Barbara; "he was ill so soon."

Harding made a slight sign of comprehension. "Well, it wouldn't be my business to say anything now," he went on in his hoarse low voice. "Besides, there is nothing to say. If the Devil had a daughter, she couldn't make any scandal out of an afternoon call in my mother's house. She couldn't suspect you of a flirtation with a death's head. Visiting the sick—it is the very pink of propriety."

Barbara felt herself continually baffled. And yet she could not accept her repulse. There was something she wanted to say to Mr. Harding, or rather, there was a word she wanted him to say to her. If he would but say it she would go, very gladly, for the walls of the room, the heavy atmosphere, and Reynold's eyes, weighed upon her like a nightmare. He had likened her once in his thoughts to a little brown-plumaged bird, and she felt like a bird that afternoon, a bird which had flown into a gloomy cage, and sat, oppressed and fascinated, with a palpitating heart. It seemed to her that his eyes had been upon her ever since she came in, and she wanted a moment's respite.

It came almost as soon as the thought had crossed her mind. Reynold coughed painfully. She started to her feet, not knowing what she ought to do, but a thin hand, lifted in the air, signed to her to be still. Presently the paroxysm subsided.

"Don't you want anything?" she ventured to ask.

He shook his head. After a moment he opened a little box on the table at his elbow, and took out a lozenge. Barbara dared not speak again. She looked at the dull, smouldering fire. "Young man," she said to herself with great distinctness, "Young man, *I think* you're dying."

She had the saddest heartache as she thought of it. That for her there should be life, London, Paris, the South—who could tell what far-off cities and shores?—who could tell how many years with Adrian? Who could tell what beauty and sweetness and music, what laughter and tears, what dreams and wonders, what joys and sorrows in days to come? While for him, this man with whom she had built castles in the air at Mitchelhurst, there were only four drab walls, a slowly burning fire, and a square grey picture of roofs and chimneys, dim in the foggy air. That was his share of the wide earth! No ease, no love, no joy, no hope,—the mother-world which was to her so bountifully kind, kept nothing for him but a few dull wintry days. Why must this be? And he was so young! And there was so much life everywhere, the earth was full of it, full to overflowing, this busy London was a surging, tumultuous sea of life about them, where they sat in that dim hushed room. She raised her head and looked timidly at the figure opposite, pale as a spectre, half lying, half lolling in his leathern chair, while he sucked his lozenge, and gazed before him with downcast eyes. From him, at least, life had ebbed hopelessly.

"Young man, I think you're dying." Oh, it was cruel, cruel! Barbara's thoughts flashed from the sick room to her own happiness—flashed home. She saw the lawn at Sandmoor, and a certain tennis-player standing in the shade of the big tulip tree, as she had seen him often that summer. He was in his white flannels, he was flushed, smiling, his grey-blue eyes were shining, he swung his racquet in his hand as he talked. He was so handsome and glad and young——ah! but no younger than Reynold Harding! Suppose it had been Adrian, and not Reynold, in the chair yonder, and her happy dreams, instead of being carried forward on the full flood of prosperity, had been left stranded and wrecked, on the low, desolate shore of death. It might have been Adrian passing thus beyond recall, the sun might have been dying out of her heaven, and at the thought she turned away her head, to hide the hot tears which welled into her eyes.

"You are sorry for me," said Reynold.

It was true, though the tears had not been for him. "I'm sorry you are ill," she said. She got up as she spoke, and stood by the fire.

"Very kind, but very useless," he answered with a smile.

"Useless!" cried little Barbara. "I know it is useless! I know I can't do anything! But, Mr. Harding, we were friends once, weren't we?"

He was silent. "I thought we were?" she faltered. "Friends—

yes, if you like. We will say that we were—friends."

"I thought we were," she repeated humbly. "I don't mean to make too much of it, but I thought we were very good friends, as people say, till that unlucky evening—that evening when you and Uncle Hayes—you were angry with me then!"

"That's a long while ago."

"It was my fault," she continued. "I didn't mean any harm, but you had a right to be vexed. And afterwards, that other evening when I went to you—I don't know what harm I did by forgetting your letter—you would not tell me, but I know you were angry. Afterwards, when I thought of it, I could see that you had been keeping it down all the time, you wouldn't reproach me then and there," said Barbara, with cheeks of flame, "but I understood when I looked back. It was only natural that you should be angry. It was very good of you not to say more."

"I think it was," said Reynold, but so indistinctly that Barbara, though she looked questioningly at him, doubted whether she heard the words.

"It would be only natural if you hated me," she went on, panting and eager, now that she had once began to speak. "But you mustn't, please, I can't bear it! I have never quarrelled with any one, never in all my life. I don't like to go away and feel that I am leaving some one behind me with whom I am not friends. So, Mr. Harding, I want you just to say that you don't hate me."

"Oh, but you are making too much of all that," he replied, and then, with an invalid's abruptness, he asked, "Where's your talisman?"

She looked down at her watch chain. "I gave it to Mr. Scarlett, he liked it," she said, with a guilty remembrance of Reynold among the brambles. "But you haven't answered me, Mr. Harding."

Her pleading was persistent, like a child's. She was childishly intent on the very word she wanted. She remembered how her uncle had laughed as she walked home after that first encounter with young Harding. "And you saw him roll into the ditch—Barbara, the poor fellow must hate you like poison!" No, he must not! It was the *word* she could not bear, it was only the *word* she knew.

"Nonsense!" he said, moving his head uneasily, "Let bygones be bygones. We can't alter the past. We are going different ways—go yours, and let me go mine in peace."

It was a harsh answer, but the frown which accompanied it betrayed irresolution as well as anger.

"I can't go so," Barbara pleaded, emboldened by this sign of possible yielding. "I never meant to do any harm. Say you are not angry—only one word—and then I'll go."

"I know you will." He laid his lean hands on the arms of his chair, and drew himself up. "Well," he said, "have it your own way—why not? What is it that I am to say?"

"Say," she began eagerly, and then checked herself. She would not ask too much. "Say only that you don't hate me," she entreated, fixing her eyes intently on his face.

"I love you, Barbara."

The girl recoiled, scared at the sudden intensity of meaning in his eyes, and in every line of his wasted figure as he leaned towards her. His hoarse whisper sent a shock through the deadened air of the drab room. Those three words had broken through the frozen silence of a life of repression and self-restraint, in them was distilled all its hoarded fierceness of love and revenge. In uttering them Reynold had uttered himself at last.

To Barbara it was as if a flash of fire showed her his passion, such a passion as her gentle soul had never imagined, against the outer darkness of death and his despair. Something choked and frightened her, and seemed to encircle her heart in its coils. It was a revelation which came from within as well as without. She threw out her hands as if he approached her. "*Adrian!*" she cried.

Reynold, leaning feebly on the arms of his chair, laughed.

"Well," he said, "are you content? I have said it."

"Oh," said Barbara, still gazing at him, "I know now—I understand—you *do* hate me!"

"Love you," he repeated. "I think I loved you from the day I saw you first. I dreamed of you at Mitchelhurst—only of you! Mitchelhurst for you, if you would have it so—but you—*you!*"

"No!" she cried.

"And afterwards you were afraid of me! If it had been any one else! But you shrank from me—you were afraid of me—the only creature in the world I loved! And then that last night when you came to me—how clever of you to discover that I was fighting with something I wanted to keep down! So I was, Barbara!"

He paused, but she only looked helplessly into his eyes.

"You don't know how hard it was," he continued meaningly. "For if I had chosen——"

"No!" she cried again.

"Yes! Do you think I did not know? *Yes!* I might have had your promise then! I might have had——"

He checked himself, but she did not attempt a second denial.

"Well, enough of this," said Reynold, after a moment. "It need not trouble you long. Look in the *Times* and you will soon see the end of it. But you can remember, if you like, that one man loved you, at any rate."

"One man does," said Barbara, in a voice which she tried to keep steady.

"Ah, the other fellow. Well, you know about that."

"Yes, I know."

"And you know that in spite of all I *don't* hate you. No, I don't, though I dare say you hate me for what I have said. But I can't help that—you asked for it."

"Yes," said Barbara. "I wish I hadn't."

"Forget it, then," he replied, with a gleam of triumph in his glance.

"You know I can't do that," she said.

She was too young to know how much may be forgotten with the help of time, and it seemed to her that Reynold's eyes would follow her to her dying day, that wherever there were shadows and silence, she would meet that reproachful, unsatisfied gaze, and hear his voice.

"You are very cruel!" she exclaimed.

"Am I?" he said more gently. "Poor child! I never meant to speak of this. I never could have spoken if you had not come this afternoon. I could not have told it to anybody but you, and you were out of my reach. Why did you come? You were quite safe if you had stayed away. You should have left me to sting myself to death in a ring of fire, as the scorpions do—or don't! What made you come inside the ring? It's narrow enough, God knows—!" he looked round as he spoke. "And you had all the world to choose from. As far as I was concerned you might have been in another planet. I couldn't have reached you. What possessed you to come here, to me? Well, you *did*, and you are stung. Is it my fault?"

"No, mine!" said the girl, passionately. "I never meant to hurt you, and you know I didn't, but it has all gone wrong from first to last. Anyhow, you have revenged yourself now. I wish—I *wish* that you were well, and strong, and rich——"

"That you might have the luxury of hating me? No, no, Barbara. I'm dying, and no one in all the world will miss me. I leave my memory to you."

He smiled as he spoke, but his utterance almost failed him, and Barbara's answer was a sob.

"I take it, then," she said in a choked voice. "Perhaps I should have been too happy if I had not known—I might never have thought about other people. But I sha'n't forget."

Then she saw that he had sunk back into his chair, and his face, which had fallen on the dull red leather, was a picture of death. The marble bust in Mitchelhurst Church did not look more bloodless.

"Oh!" said Barbara, "you are tired!"

"Mortally," he replied, faintly unclosing his lips. "Good-bye."

She paused for an instant, looking at the dropped lids which hid those eyes that she had feared. She could do nothing for him but leave him. "Good-bye," she said, very softly, as if she feared to disturb his rest, and then she went away.

The window on the stairs was a dim grey shape. Barbara groped her way down, and stood hesitating in the passage. It was really only half a minute before the maid came up from the basement with matches to light the gas, but it was like an age of dreary perplexity.

"I've just left Mr. Harding," she said hurriedly to the girl, whose matter-of-fact face was suddenly illuminated by the jet of flame. "I'm afraid he's tired. I think somebody ought to go to him."

"Mind the step, miss," was the reply. "I'll tell missis. I dare say he'll have his cocoa, I think it's past the time."

"Oh, *don't* wait for me!" cried Barbara. "I'm all right."

She felt as if Reynold Harding might die by his fireside while she was being ceremoniously shown out. She reached the door first and shut it quickly after her, to cut all attentions short. She had hurried out at the gate, under the foggy outline of a little laburnum, when a shout from the pursuing cabman aroused her to the consciousness that she had started off to walk.

Thus arrested, she got into the hansom, covered with confusion, and not daring to look at the man as she gave her address. He must certainly think that she meant to cheat him, or that she was mad. She shrank back into the seat, feeling sure that he would look through the little hole in the roof, from time to time, to see what his eccentric fare might be doing, and she folded her hands and sat very still, to impress him with the idea that she had become quite sane and well-behaved. As if it mattered what the cabman thought! And yet she blushed over her blunder while Reynold Harding's "I love you," was still sounding in her ears, and while the hansom rolled southward through the lamp-lit, glimmering streets, to the tune of *Barbara Allen.*

CHAPTER X

JANUARY, 1883.

"A train of human memories,

Crying: The past must never pass away."

"They depart and come no more,

Or come as phantoms and as ghosts."

"When we are married," Adrian had said on that blissful day in Nutfield Lane, "before we go abroad, before we go *anywhere*, we will run down to Mitchelhurst for a day, won't we?"

Barbara had agreed to this, as she would have agreed to anything he had suggested, and the plan had been discussed during the summer months, till it seemed to have acquired a kind of separate existence, as if Adrian's light whim had been transformed into Destiny. The bleak little English village stood in the foreground of their radiant honeymoon picture of Paris and the south. The straggling rows of cottages, the cabbage plots, the churchyard where the damp earth, heavy with its burden of death, rose high against the buttressed wall, the blacksmith's forge with its fierce rush of sparks, the *Rothwell Arms* with the sign that swung above the door—were all strangely distinct against a bright confusion of far-off stir and gaiety, white foreign streets, and skies and waters of deepest blue. All their lives, if they pleased, for that world beyond, but the one day, first, for Mitchelhurst.

Thus it happened that the careless fancy of April was fulfilled in January. January is a month which exhibits most English scenery to small advantage; and Mitchelhurst wore its dreariest aspect when a fly from the county town drew up beneath the swaying sign. The little holiday couple, stepping out of it into the midst of the universal melancholy, looked somewhat out of place. Adrian and Barbara had that radiant consciousness of having done something very remarkable indeed which characterises newly-married pairs. They had the usual conviction that an exceptional perfection in their union made it the very flower of all love in all time. They had plucked this supremely delicate felicity, and here they were, alighting with it from the shabby conveyance, and standing in the prosaic dirt of Mitchelhurst Street. The sign gave a long, discordant creak by way of greeting, and they started and looked up.

"It wouldn't be worse for a little grease," the landlord allowed, in a voice which was not much more melodious than the creaking sign.

Scarlett laughed, but he realised the whole scene with an amusement which had a slight flavour of dismay. Was this the place which was to give his honeymoon an added touch of poetry? How poor and ignoble the houses were! How bare and bleak the outlines of the landscape! How low the dull, grey roof of sky! How raw the January wind upon his cheek! There was only a momentary pause. Barbara was looking down the well-known road, the bullet-headed landlord scratched his unshaven chin, and the disconsolate chickens came nearer and nearer, pecking aimlessly among the puddles.

"I suppose you can give us some luncheon?" said the young man, and in the interest of that important question it hardly seemed as if there had been a pause at all.

The landlady arrived in a flurry, asking what they would please to order, and Adrian and she kept up a brisk dialogue for the next five minutes. Finally, it was decided that they should have chops. Perhaps the discussion satisfied some traditional sense of what was the right thing to do on arriving at an inn. There was nothing to have *but* the chops which Adrian had chosen, and he murmured something of "fixed fate, free-will" under his moustache, as he crossed the road in the direction of the church.

"In an hour," he said. "That will give us time to see the church and the village. Then, after luncheon, we will go to the old Place, and the fly shall call for us there, and take us back the short way. Will that do, Barbara?"

Of course it would do; and when they reached the churchyard she bade him wait a moment and she would get the key. The stony path to Mrs. Spearman's cottage was curiously familiar—the broken palings, the pump, the leafless alder-bush. The only difference was that it was Barbara Scarlett—a different person—who was stepping over the rough pebbles.

She returned to Adrian, who was leaning against the gate-post.

"Mitchelhurst isn't very beautiful," he said, with an air of conviction. "I thought I remembered it, but it has come upon me rather as a shock. Somehow, I fancied—Barbara, is it possible that I have taken all the beauty out of it—that it belongs to *me* now, instead of to Mitchelhurst? Can that be?"

She smiled her answer to the question, and then—

"I think it looks very much as usual," she said, gazing dispassionately round. "Of course, it is prettier in the spring—or in the summer. It was summer when you came, you know."

She had a vague recollection of having pleaded the cause of Mitchelhurst at some other time in the same way, which troubled her a little.

"Yes, I know it was summer," said Adrian. "But still——"

"You mustn't say anything against Mitchelhurst," cried Barbara, swinging her great key. "It isn't beautiful, but I feel as if I belonged to it, somehow. It changed me, I can't tell why or how, but it did. After I had been six months with Uncle Hayes, I went home for a fortnight in the spring, and everything seemed so different. It was all so bright and busy there, everybody talked so fast about little everyday things, and the rooms were so small and crowded. I suppose it was because I had been living with echoes and old pictures in that great house. Louisa and Hetty were always having little secrets and jokes, there wasn't any harm in them, you know, but I felt as if I could not care about them or laugh at them, and yet some of them had been my jokes, before I went to Mitchelhurst. And I could not make them understand why I cared about the Rothwells and their pictures, when I had never known any of them."

"Louisa is a very nice girl," said Scarlett; "but if Mitchelhurst is all the difference between you two, I am bound to say that I have a high opinion of the place."

"Well, I don't know any other difference."

"Don't you?" and he smiled as he followed her along the churchyard path. "No other difference? None?" He smiled, and yet he knew that the old house had given a charm to Barbara when he saw her first. She had been like a little damask rose, breathing and glowing against its grim walls. He took the key from her hand, and turned it in the grating lock.

It seemed as if the very air were unchanged within, so heavy and still it was. Barbara went forward, and her little footfalls were hardly audible on the matting. Adrian, with his head high, sniffed in search of a certain remembered perfume, as of mildewed hymn-books, found it, and was content. It brought back to him, as only an odour could, his first afternoon in the church, when he stood with one of those books in his hand, and watched the Rothwell pew which held Barbara.

Having enjoyed his memory he faced round and inspected St. Michael, who was as new, and neat, and radiant as ever. Adrian speculated how long it would take to make him look a little less of a parvenu. "Would a couple of centuries do him any good, I wonder?" he mused, half-aloud. "Not much, I fear." The archangel returned his gaze with a permanent serenity which seemed to imply that a century more or less was a matter of indifference to his dragon and him.

Barbara had gone straight to the Rothwell monuments, where Scarlett presently joined her. She did not take her eyes from the tombs, but she stole a warm little hand under his arm. "I wish he could have been buried here," she said in a low voice.

Reynold had said that he bequeathed her his memory, but now, in her happiness, it seemed to be receding, fading, melting away. She gazed helplessly in remorseful pain; he was only a chilly phantom; the very fierceness of his passion was but a dying spark of fire. She could recall his words, but they were dull and faint, like echoes nearly spent. She could not recall their meaning—that was gone. The declaration of love which had burst upon her like a great wave, filling her with pity and wonder and fear, had ebbed to some unapproachable distance, leaving her perplexed and half incredulous. Adrian, in flesh and blood, was at her side, and she thrilled and glowed at his touch; but when she thought of Reynold Harding she met only a vague emptiness. He was not with the Rothwells in this quiet corner; he was not where she had left him, lying back in his leathern chair. That room was swept and garnished and cold, as he had said. No doubt they had put him in some suburban cemetery, some wilderness of graves which to her was only a name of dreariness. Standing where he had once stood in Mitchelhurst Church, she only felt his absence, and she thought that she could have recalled him better if he had been at rest beneath the dimly-lettered pavement on which her eyes were fixed.

She was wrong. Memories cannot bear the outer air, or be laid away in the cold earth; they can only live when they are hidden in our hearts, and quickened by our pulses. Barbara could not keep the remembrance of Reynold's love alive, with no love of her own to warm it. But in her ignorance she said, wistfully—

"I wish he could have been buried here!" and then added in a quicker tone, "I suppose you'll say it makes no difference where he lies."

"Indeed I sha'n't," said Adrian. "There may be beauty or ugliness, fitness or unfitness, in one's last home as well as any other. Yes, I wish he were here. But he was an unlucky fellow; it seemed as if he were never to have anything he wanted, didn't it?"

"How do you mean—not anything?"

"Well, I think he would have liked Mitchelhurst Place."

"Yes," said Barbara, "he would, I know."

"And I am sure he would have liked the name of Rothwell. He was ashamed of his father's people. That pork-butcher rankled."

"Oh!" said Barbara, still looking at the tombs, "did you know about that? Did everybody know?" She spoke very softly, as if she thought the dusty Rothwell, peering out of his marble curls, might overhear. "No, I suppose he didn't like him."

"I know he didn't. Well, he hadn't the name he liked: he was saddled with the pork-butcher's name. And then, worst of all, he couldn't have you, Barbara!"

She turned upon him with parted lips and a startled face.

"Well," said Scarlett, "he couldn't, you know."

"Adrian! how did you know he cared for me? He did, but how did you know it? I thought I ought not to tell anybody."

"I saw him once," said Scarlett, "and I found it out. I saw him again—just passed him in the road, and we did not say a word. But I was doubly sure, if that were possible. Poor devil! If he could have had his way we should not have met in the lane that day, Barbara."

"I never dreamed of it," she said. "I thought he hated me."

"If a girl thinks a man hates her," said Adrian, "I suppose the chances are he does one thing or the other."

"I never dreamed of it," she repeated, "never, till he told me at the end. It could not be my fault, could it, as I did not know? But it seemed so cruel—so hard! He had cared for me all the time, he said, and nobody had ever cared for him."

"You mustn't be unhappy about that," said Scarlett, gently.

"But that's just it!" Barbara exclaimed, plaintively. "I ought to be unhappy, and I can't be. Adrian! I've got all the happiness—a whole world full of it—and he had none. I must be a heartless wretch to stand here, and think of him, and be so glad because——"

Because her hand was on Adrian's arm.

"My darling," he said, in a tone half tenderly jesting, half earnest, "you mustn't blame yourself for this. What had you to do with it? Do you think you could have made that poor fellow happy?"

She looked at him perplexed.

"He loved me," she said.

"I know he did. You might have given him a momentary rapture if you had loved him. But make him happy—not you! Not anybody, Barbara! How could you look at his face, and not see that he carried his unhappiness about with him? I verily believe that there was no place on the earth's surface where he could have been at peace. Underneath it—perhaps!"

Barbara sighed, looking down at the stones.

"You people with consciences blame yourselves for things foredoomed," said Scarlett. "Harding's destiny was written before you were born, my dear child. Besides," he added, in a lighter tone, "what would you do with the pair of us?"

"That's true," she said, thoughtfully.

"Take my word for it," he went on, "if you want to do any good you should give happiness to the people who are fit for it. You can brighten my life—oh, my darling, you don't know how much! But his—never! If you were an artist you might as well spend your best work in painting angels and roses on the walls of the family vault down here as try it."

"Yes," said Barbara. Then, after a pause, she spoke with a kind of sob in her voice, "But if one had thrown in just a flower before the door was shut! I couldn't, you know, I hadn't anything to give him!"

Scarlett, by way of answer, laid his hand on hers. When you come face to face with such an undoubted fact as the attraction a man's lonely suffering has for a woman, argument is useless. It is an ache for which self-devotion is the only relief. He perfectly understood the remorseful workings of Barbara's tender heart.

"I couldn't do without you, my dear," he said.

"Oh, Adrian!—no!" she exclaimed. "That day when I said good-bye to him, he fancied I was crying for him once, and even that was for you. I was just thinking, if it had been you sitting there!"

"Foolish child! I'm not to be got rid of so easily."

"Don't talk of it!" said Barbara.

Her hand tightened on his arm, and she looked up at him, with a glance that said plainly that the sun would drop out of her sky if any mischance befell him.

"Well," she said, after a minute, more in her ordinary voice, as if she were dismissing Reynold Harding from the conversation, "I'm glad you know. I wanted you to know, but of course I could not tell you."

"It's wonderful with women," said Adrian, gliding easily into generalities, "the things they *don't* think it necessary to tell us, taking it for granted that we know them, and we *can't* know them and *don't* know them to our dying day—

and the things they *do* think it necessary to tell us, with elaborate precautions and explanations—which we knew perfectly well from the first."

"Oh, is that it?" Barbara replied, smartly. "Then I shall tell you everything, and you can be surprised or not as you please."

"I sha'n't be much surprised," said Adrian, "unless, perhaps, you tell me something when you think you are not telling anything at all."

And with this they went off together to look at the seat in which he sat when Barbara saw him first, and then she stood in her old place in the Rothwells' red-lined pew, and looked across at him, recalling that summer Sunday. It would have been a delightful amusement if the church had been a few degrees warmer, but Barbara could not help shivering a little, and Adrian frankly avowed that he found it impossible to maintain his feelings at the proper pitch.

"I'm blue," he said, "and I'm iced, and I can't be sentimental. And you wore a thin cream-coloured dress that day, which is terrible to think of. Might write something afterwards, perhaps," he continued, musingly. "Not while my feet are like two stones, but I feel as if I might thaw into a sonnet, or something of the kind."

Barbara looked up at him reverentially, and Adrian began to laugh.

"Let's go and eat those chops," he said.

Later, as they walked along the street towards Mitchelhurst Place, Scarlett was silent for a time, glancing right and left at the dull cottages. Here and there one might catch a glimpse of firelight through the panes, but most of them were drearily blank, with grey windows and closed doors. It was too cold for the straw-plaiters to stand on their thresholds and gossip while they worked. There was a foreshadowing of snow in the low-hanging clouds.

"What are you thinking of?" Barbara asked him.

"Don't let us ever come here again!" he answered. "It's all very well for this once; we are young enough, we have our happiness before us. But never again! Suppose we were old and sad when we came back, or suppose——" He stopped short. "Suppose one came back alone," should have been the ending of that sentence.

"Very well," she agreed hastily, as if to thrust aside the unspoken words.

"We say our good-bye to Mitchelhurst to-day, then?" Adrian insisted.

"Yes. There won't be any temptation to come again, if what they told us is true—will there?"

She referred to a rumour which they had heard at the *Rothwell Arms*, that as Mr. Croft could not find a tenant for the Place he meant to pull it down.

"No," said Scarlett. "It seems a shame, though," he added.

Presently they came in sight of the entrance—black bars, and beyond them a stirring of black boughs in the January wind, over the straight, bleak roadway to the house. The young man pushed the gate. "Some one has been here to-day," he said, noting a curve already traced on the damp earth.

"Some one to take the house, perhaps," Barbara suggested. "Look, there's a carriage waiting out to the right of the door. I wish they hadn't happened to choose this very day. I would rather have had the old Place to ourselves, wouldn't you?"

"Much," said Adrian.

These young people were still in that ecstatic mood in which, could they have had the whole planet to themselves, it would never have occurred to them that it was lonely. Their eyes met as they answered, and if at that moment the wind-swept avenue had been transformed into sunlit boughs of blossoming orange, they might not have remarked any accession of warmth and sweetness.

The old woman who was in charge recognised Barbara, and made no difficulty about allowing them to wander through the rooms at their leisure. In fact, she was only too glad not to leave her handful of fire on such a chilly errand.

"Is it true," Mrs. Scarlett asked eagerly, "that Mr. Croft is going to pull the house down?"

"So they tell me, ma'am. There's to be a sale here, come Midsummer, and after that they say the old Place comes down. There's nobody to take it now poor Mr. Hayes is gone."

Adrian's glance quickened at the mention of a sale, and then he recalled his expressed intention never to come to Mitchelhurst again. "Perhaps he'll find a tenant before then," he said. "You've got somebody here to-day, haven't you?"

The woman started in sudden remembrance. "Oh, there's a lady," she said, "I most forgot her. She said she was one of the old family, and used to live here. My orders are to go round with 'em when they come to look at the house, but the lady didn't want nobody, she said, she knew her way, and she walked right off.

"I hope it ain't nothing wrong, but she's been gone some time."

"I should think it was quite right," said Scarlett. "Come, Barbara."

They went from room to room. All were silent, empty, and cold, with shutters partly unclosed, letting in slanting gleams of grey light. The painted eyes of the portraits on the wall looked askance at them as they stood gazing about. All the little modern additions which Mr. Hayes had made to the furniture for comfort's sake had been taken away, and the Rothwells had come into possession of their own again.

Scarlett opened the old piano as he passed. "Do you remember?" he said, glancing brightly, and with a smile curving his red lips, as he began, with one hand, to touch a familiar tune. But Barbara cried "Hush!" and the tinkling, jangling notes died suddenly into the stillness. "Suppose she were to hear!"

"I wonder where she is," he rejoined, with a glance round. "She must have come to say good-bye to her old home, too."

There was no sign of her as they crossed the hall (where Barbara's great clock had long ago run down) and went up the wide, white stairs. But it was curious how they felt her unseen presence, and how the knowledge that at any moment they might turn a corner and encounter that living woman, made the place more truly haunted than if it had held a legion of ghosts. They walked in silence, like a couple of half-frightened children, along the passages, and the remembrance that the old house was doomed was with them all the time. It was strange to lay their warm light hands on those strong walls, which had outlasted so many lives, so much hope, and so much hopelessness, and to think that they, in their fragile, happy existence might well remain when Mitchelhurst Place was forgotten. It seemed hardly more than a phantom house already.

"I almost think she must have gone," Barbara whispered, as they came downstairs again.

"No," said Adrian, with an oblique glance which her eyes followed.

Kate Harding was standing by one of the windows in the entrance hall, a stately figure in heavy draperies of black. Hearing the steps of the intruders she turned slightly, and partially confronted them, and the light fell on her face, pale and proud, close-lipped, full of mute and dreary defiance. Only she herself knew the passionate eagerness with which, as a girl, she had renounced her old home—only she knew the strange power with which Mitchelhurst had drawn her back once more. Fate had been too strong for her, and she had returned to her own place, perhaps to the thought of the son who had belonged more to it than to her. Her presence there that day was a confession of defeat too bitter to be spoken, a last homage of farewell to the old house which she was not rich enough to save.

Her eyes, resting indifferently on the girl's face, widened in sudden recognition, and she looked from Barbara to Adrian. Her glance enveloped the young couple in its swift intensity, and then fell coldly to the pavement as she bent her head. Barbara blushed and drooped, Scarlett bowed, as they passed the motionless woman, drawn back a little against the wall, with the faded map of the great Mitchelhurst estate hanging just behind her.

Their fly was waiting at the door, and in less than a minute they were rolling quickly down the avenue. Adrian, stooping to tuck a rug about his wife's feet, only raised himself in time to catch a last glimpse of the white house front, and to cry, "Good-bye, Mitchelhurst!" Barbara echoed his good-bye. Mitchelhurst was only an episode in her life; she cared for the place, yet she was not sorry to escape from its shadows of loves and hates, too deep and dark for her, and its unconquerable melancholy. She left it, but a touch of its sadness would cling to her in after years, giving her the tenderness which comes from a sense— dim, perhaps, but all-pervading—of the underlying suffering of the world. She looked back and saw her happiness tossed lightly and miraculously from crest to crest of the black waves which might have engulfed it in a moment; and even as she leaned in the warm shelter of Adrian's arm, she was sorry for the lives that were wrecked, and broken, and forgotten.

"Look!" he said quickly, as the road wound along the hill-side, and a steep bank, crowned with leafless thorns and brown stunted oaks, rose on the right, "this is where I said good-bye to you, Barbara, and you never knew it!"

"Never!" she cried. "No, I thought you had gone away, and hadn't cared to say good-bye."

"Well, you were kinder to me than you knew. You left me a bunch of red berries lying in the road."

"Ah, but if I had known you were there!"

"Why," said Adrian, "you wouldn't have left me anything at all. You would have died first! You know you would! It was better as it was."

"Perhaps," she allowed.

"Anyhow, it is best as it is," said he conclusively, and to that she agreed; but her smile was followed by a quick little sigh.

"What does that mean?" he demanded, tenderly.

"Nothing," she said, "nothing, *really*."

It was nothing. Only, absorbed in picturing Adrian's mute farewell, she had passed the place where she first saw Reynold Harding, and had not spared him one thought as she went by. And she was never coming to Mitchelhurst again.

THE END.

Clay and Taylor, Printers, Bungay, Suffolk.

www.ingramcontent.com/pod-product-compliance
Lightning Source LLC
Chambersburg PA
CBHW020809020726
47495CB00008B/2657